THE SWEET TALKER

CATHRYN FOX

COPYRIGHT

The Sweet Talker

The Sweet Talker
Copyright 2021 by Cathryn Fox
Published by Cathryn Fox

ISBN Ebook: 978-1-989374-39-9

ISBN Print: 978-1-989374-38-2

1

BRODY

Six days until Christmas Eve:

"Why do I feel like I just drove straight onto the set of a Hallmark movie?" I ask my buddy Declan as I look through my dirty windshield and take in the decked-out shops lining Main Street. Thank God I don't have epilepsy. All the flashing lights in the store windows, not to mention the sparkling spruce wreaths hanging from every lamppost, are liable to trigger a damn seizure.

I slow my sports car on the slushy streets of Holiday Peak, Massachusetts, the sugary sweet town Declan calls home. Talk about a community taking Christmas to the extreme, and no, I'm not secretly enjoying the festive energy bubbling up around me. Not much, anyway.

"Watch a lot of Hallmark movies, do you?" Declan asks, busting my balls, and why wouldn't he? Do you know any guys that blurt shit out about Hallmark movies, like they're totally into them? Didn't think so.

I glance at my buddy as he stares out the window, nostalgia all over his face. Declan and I became close when I joined the Seattle Shooters defensive line up a couple of years ago. He took me under his wing, and we've been tight ever since. While he knows a lot about me, more than most, he doesn't need to know I'm a sucker for a good Christmas movie, which undoubtedly stems from far too many craptastic Christmases over the years.

He tears his gaze from the festive streets, and his brow arches in challenge as he waits for me to answer. "So that's a yes? You watch a lot of Hallmark movies?"

"Sometimes I'm too lazy to stretch for the remote," I say, rubbing my eyes. The drive from my place in Boston to Declan's hometown isn't a long one. I'm just tired from kicking ass during our winning game against Detroit two nights ago and I'm damn well looking forward to this break.

"Which means you were already watching the Women's Network, correct?" He grins. "Look I don't care, just stop denying it."

I shake my head. Leave it to Declan to call me on my shit. Every. Single. Time. I lift my chin. "You don't know my life," I shoot back. I hide a grin and add, "Sometimes those movies are on the Lifetime channel, you know." We both laugh at that. Yeah, I get it. Hours spent watching chick flicks hardly fits my image, and it's best that information doesn't leave this car. While I might be known as the Sweet Talker—and I'm not being cocky when I say this, but I'm pretty good at scoring with the ladies—on the ice, I'm a pit bull with one job: keep the opponents from scoring. But enough of that. I need a change of subject before Declan makes me cash in my man card.

"Do I really have to bring a date to Christmas Eve dinner?" I ask with a groan as I sink deeper into the driver's seat. To be honest, I'm a little played out, and agreed to join Declan for Christmas because he grew up in a sleepy town with a nearby ski hill, and I need downtime. That, and my father, an NHL hall of famer, couldn't care less about seeing his kid over the holidays. He's too busy with wife number five, or maybe it's six, and don't even get me started on my biological mother. But sometimes I think I worked so hard at hockey just to get his attention, his approval. You'd think he'd be proud of his son following in his footsteps. I guess he's too self-centered and interested in his own pleasures to care.

Declan shrugs. "Up to you, but like I said, no one sits alone at Mom's table. If the chair next to you is empty, she'll fill it with my cousin Eugenie, and that woman..." He gives a low slow whistle. "Let's just say she's a huge Brody Tucker fan, and I'm pretty sure she wants you to be her baby daddy."

I laugh out loud, holding one hand up. "I draw the line there, bro."

"I know you do, so you better put a plan together and find someone to fill that chair, before Mom does and you find out you're Houdini Eugenie's baby daddy before you even realize you've been unzipped."

"Note to self, steer clear of Houdini Eugenie." Snow starts falling again, and I turn on my wipers, spreading a streak of dirty slush across my window. Way to mess up my visibility. I scrunch to look through a clean streak. "Where am I going to find a date this late, anyway?"

"You have six days."

I consider that for a moment. "I guess that's plenty of time to sweet talk a girl into a fancy dinner at your parents' place." Declan snorts, shaking his head. "What?" I ask.

"Maybe the women in Holiday Peak won't fall for your charm." He taps his head. "They're kind of smart like that around these parts."

I tap the steering wheel and grin. "Guess I won't know if I don't try."

"Just don't try it with Nikki," he says, a warning in his voice. "I don't want her getting mixed up with the likes of you."

"You're the one they call Heartbreaker, not me, and it's not like you have any claim on her. All you do is hang out when you're home and then return to the team in a shit mood. If you like her, do something about it."

"It's not like that." He exhales, averting my gaze, but not before I catch the frown on his forehead. I'm not exactly sure what the deal is with him and Nikki. I guess I'll never know because he shuts down whenever her name comes up.

"Who should I ask, then?" I scan the sidewalk, looking for possible candidates. A pretty brunette walks by and I perk up, until I notice the little boy by her side. Nope. Not her. Moving along. It's not that I have anything against kids. Simply put, relationships never work out for me, and no way do I want to drag a kid into my world only to screw him up when I eventually screw up. I don't want to be the cause of anyone's therapy. He's better off never having known me on a personal level.

Declan pulls his phone from his pocket and sends a text. He seems a bit distracted when he says, "Are you suggesting I pick someone for you?"

"This is your town, isn't it? You know the women better than I do, and maybe Nikki has a friend. Just point the way." I offer him my best smile. "I'll take care of the rest."

"Let me get this straight. You're saying whoever I pick, you can charm to the table?"

"Is that a challenge?"

He stares at his phone for a second, shoves it into his pocket and looks at me. "Maybe."

I toss him a cocky grin. Being a star in the NHL comes with its perks—Declan knows that firsthand. You know what being a star in the NHL doesn't come with? Long term relationships. At least not for me. Lots of my buddies have fallen in love and are now married with kids. But the only thing I know about love is how to mess it up, which is why I no longer try.

"Try me, bro. Pick a girl and I'll get her to the table." I flick on the windshield washer, but no fluid comes out. "I can't see a thing."

"Wait, pull over."

"What?"

"Right here," he practically shouts. "Stop the car."

I jerk the car to the right, and my suspension squeals as my front right tire plunges into a slush covered pothole near the curb. The god-awful screeching sound is followed by a gasp so loud it drowns out the song on the radio. My heart jumps into my throat. "What the hell?"

"Oh, shit." Declan jerks his thumb to the right. "You just soaked someone."

Worry races through me as I kill the ignition and jump from the car. Circling the front, my eyes go wide when my gaze lands on a girl around my age—late twenties. It's a bit hard to tell exactly how old she is as she stands there gasping for air, cold, wet slushy snow dripping from her—compliments of my erratic driving.

"I'm so sorry," I blurt out, thankful that I hadn't done more damage, like actually hit her. "Declan, grab me something." As Declan goes to the trunk, I take in the woman trying to catch her breath as she swipes wet, dirty snow from her face. I scan the length of her. Christ, I don't think there's an inch of her that I missed. "I'm so sorry," I say again. "Let me help you."

"No thanks. I think you've done enough already," she shoots back, a cold shiver wracking her body. Okay, she's upset because I soaked her. I can understand that, and maybe she was headed somewhere important, and needed to be, well... dry. Despite her protest, I take my coat off and hold it out to her as Declan comes back with one of our team towels. He spreads it open, and she takes the towel and wipes her face. "Thank you," she says quietly to Declan.

"Here, take my coat," I say.

She hands the towel back to Declan, shaking her head at me. "I'm fine."

Clearly, she's not fine, but I'm not about to call her on that as she averts my gaze and scans the snowbank. "Let me make it up to you." I reach for my wallet. "I'll pay for the dry cleaning."

She holds her hand out, palm facing me. "I don't want your money."

"Please, let me do something to make this up to you. Dinner? New clothes?" She toys with the zipper on her winter jacket. "Axe throwing?" I glance up and down the streets. Maybe they don't have that here.

Her head lifts and she glares at me like I might have just escaped an institution. Maybe under the circumstances, with her soaked and freezing, I can understand how axe throwing was a little bit out there.

"Keep the money." She wrings out her ponytail, and that's when I notice the pretty green flecks in her dark brown eyes. "Maybe you could use it for driving lessons."

I bite back a wince as Declan stifles a chuckle. She looks down again, searches the snowbank. A thunderous noise rumbles down the street and I jump back, pulling my new friend—or rather enemy—with me, before the snowplow soaks us both. The plow drops its blade at the front of my car and scrapes up the snow.

"Great," she says under her breath, and I examine the layer of packed snow with her, even though I have no idea what it is I'm looking for.

"Did you lose something?"

She briefly closes her eyes, like she's trying to convince herself murder is wrong, and then says, "No, I just like to search snowbanks for fun. It's a pasttime here in Holiday Peak, something you out of towners wouldn't know anything about."

"How do you know I'm from out of town?"

She arches a brow glancing at my sports car, which isn't ideal for this mountainous town. *Alrighty then*. People on the street slow as they see us, a few pointing at Declan and me with recognition. "Can I drop you somewhere?" I gesture toward my car.

"No."

"Maybe you could call someone to pick you up. Do you have a boyfriend or husband I could call?"

I'm not hitting on her—I don't think. It's just that she looks a bit traumatized, and might need someone other than me coming to her rescue.

"No."

I really don't know why my chest loosened at that answer. We're different people from different worlds, and yeah, I can't forget her instant dislike of me, and maybe even my car.

"You should probably get inside before you freeze to death," I suggest.

Her head lifts. Speaking of death... As her murderous eyes turn on me, I'm pretty sure she's thinking about ways to bury me in the slushy snow, or maybe she's reconsidering the axe throwing, with me as her target. "You think?" she shoots back.

Clearly, we're off to a good start.

"I'm sorry. Look. Can we start again?"

"You can keep the towel," Declan says, holding it out for her. She looks at the Seattle Shooters emblem, and her eyes lift. She smiles for the first time, and my heart stills a little in my chest. Jesus, she's gorgeous—when she's not contemplating killing me, that is. "Declan Bradbury. I've heard a lot about you. You're famous in this town, and it's nice to meet you in person."

"Nice to meet you too, and you are...?"

"Freezing to death. Thanks to your friend." She searches the snow again, and her teeth clatter a little louder.

I step closer, crowd her, wanting to offer her my warmth but afraid of getting a knee to the nuts. As I crowd her, I breathe in her delicious scent. Cookies and cream and...chocolate. Not just any chocolate. No, she smells like the expensive kind my third stepmother used to put out at Christmas—before she disappeared from my life, taking a little bit of my heart with her.

"I can help you find whatever it is you're looking for," I offer.

She stares at the plow as it takes a turn, and for a second I think she might cry. But the anger is back in her eyes when she turns to me. "I don't...need your help...you've..." Choppy words through clattering teeth fall off as a shop door opens behind her, a little bell ringing to alert the staff to a customer.

"Done enough, I know." Feeling like total crap, I adjust my ballcap as she turns, disappearing into the shop. The delectable scent of warm gooey chocolate fills the street, as the door falls shut behind her.

I stand there for a moment, a little confused at her sudden departure. Then again, it's possible she was on the brink of hypothermia. I put my jacket back on, reading the sign above the door: The Chocolate Lab. I guess she must work there.

"You been here five whole minutes, and look at you, making friends," Declan says.

I turn to my buddy, and shrug. "Who the hell was that, anyway?

He looks past my shoulders up and down the street. "I don't know."

"Don't you know everyone in this town?"

"She must be new around here. That shop wasn't here last time I was home."

His mouth turns up at the corner, presenting me with those double dimples that drive women wild. "Axe throwing?"

"Cut me some slack, I panicked, and what the hell is the matter with you? Why are you smiling like the village idiot?"

"Because I pick her." He points to the chocolate shop. "She's the girl you have to charm to the dinner table."

I scoff. "Oh, hell no. She's a man-hater."

"I don't know if I'd say that. I thought she was rather sweet." My jaw drops and he continues with, "She knew who I was and smiled at me."

"Then you date her."

He shoves his hands into his pockets, and rolls one shoulder. "No, I think I'll leave that to you."

I cover my crotch. "I'm kind of fond of these guys, Declan, and wouldn't mind them intact when I leave here after Christmas."

He laughs. "Then I guess you have your work cut out for you."

"My work cut out for me? No, my friend, getting her to the table isn't going to take work, it's going to take a Christmas miracle."

"Are you saying you can't do it? That the infamous Sweet Talker can't sweet talk his way into any woman's life?" He turns and heads down the street, stopping outside a coffee shop.

I make a move to go when my foot knocks something loose in the snow. I glanced down and spot something shiny lodged between the bank and a lamppost. I snatch the object up, and the second I realize what I'm holding, a wide smile crosses my face.

"Not saying that at all," I shoot back.

He pulls open the coffee shop door, pausing to look back at me. "Then it's on?"

I grin, as I shove my ticket to winning this challenge into my pocket. "It's already done."

2

JOSIE

I step into the warmth of my shop, the delicious scent of chocolate doing little to soothe the deep-seated pain that lives inside of me as my assistant Kayley takes one look at me and gasps.

"Are you okay?" Wiping her hands on a cloth, she comes out from behind the counter to get a better look at me. Stupid tears prick my eyes, and I try to fight them back as I hold my hand up to wave her off, like what just happened out on the street was nothing more than an unfortunate incident. But it wasn't an unfortunate incident. Not to me. No, to me I'd just lost a huge part of my soul in that snowbank, and nothing or no one can bring it back now.

"It was an accident," I say, working to push down my anguish and hating myself for the way I treated a complete stranger. Mr. Pothole, or whatever his name was, never meant any harm, and he definitely didn't drive into that puddle on purpose. I hold one finger up in front of Kayley's worried face. "Pothole, one." My thumb and index form a circle.

"Josie, zero." I struggle to project my best happy voice despite the storm going on inside me.

Another customer enters the store as she shoos me away. "Go get changed, I've got this."

With little choice in the matter, I nod, walking to the back of the chocolate shop, thankful that my apartment is above it and I don't need to go outside again. I was on my way to Coffee Klatch to grab a couple of lattes for Kayley and me—Christmas time is crazy busy at the shop, giving us little time for breaks—when I accidently dropped my phone into a snowbank.

I was seconds from fishing it from the slush when I was assaulted by a cold puddle. Some might say after that incident, the rest of the day could only go uphill, right? Heck, right up until that moment, I tried to be one of those positive people—despite the pain I'd been through over the last year. But this time, I couldn't summon any glass-half-full attitude. Watching that plow drop its blade, and undoubtedly scoop up my phone and carry it away, sliced my already wounded heart in two. I'm surprised I didn't bleed out on the ground. I know, I know, you're probably thinking, it's just a phone, it's replaceable. You'd be right. The one thing that's not replaceable, however, is the voice message my late husband sent me last year before he passed away.

I haven't been able to bring myself to listen to it, and that's why I packed up my store in Boston, moving to Holiday Peak. A fresh start. A fresh town. A fresh—or rather not so fresh—puddle of dirty slush in the face, and everywhere else.

"I'll be right back," I say to Kayley, pretending to brush remnants of snow from my face. It's a week from Christmas, the holiday spirit is high here in Holiday Peak, and tears are the last thing anyone needs to see. I'm not a girl to bring anyone down. Before I can make it to the back room, the bell over the door jingles and I spin, half expecting to see Mr. Pothole. My gut clenches as the town's sheriff, Patrick McCullum walks in. His eyes go wide at my disarrayed state.

"Josie, what happened?"

"Fight with a pothole, the pothole won," I explain. Maybe if he sees me like this, he'll stop asking me out. He's a nice man, as sweet as can be, but I'm just not attracted to him. Not that I'd go out with him even if I did like him. That would dishonor my late husband's memory. Since it's not in my nature to hurt anyone, a couple of months back, I told a little-white lie, just to preserve his feelings. I point to the back steps. "I'm just going to go get changed."

"Yes, go. Wouldn't want your boyfriend showing up for the holidays seeing you like this. He'd think we weren't taking good care of you in this town." The fine lines below his eyes crinkle, a light dusting of snow in his salt and pepper hair. As I take in his smile, there is a part of me that suspects he doesn't believe I have a boyfriend in Boston. He'd be right. Who knows, as a sheriff, maybe he even did a bit of digging.

"He would never think that. He knows how much I love Holiday Peak."

His brows raise. "He is coming for the holidays, right? I'm looking forward to meeting him."

"Yeah, uh sure, that's the plan. I'd better go get changed."

As I head up the steps, I berate myself for lying. Nothing good can come from it, and now I'm caught in a web of deceit, with Patrick expecting my boyfriend to visit over Christmas. As I scold myself for that fib, my thoughts switch to my behavior on the street. I was upset and angry, not so much at being soaked, but at the loss of my phone. I never should have taken my troubles out on Mr. Pothole. He offered to make things right, pay for dry cleaning, buy me dinner, and weirdly, take me axe throwing. Strange, but nice, and there was something about his eyes—a kindness in them that really caught me off guard—that drew me in. That could also be why I lashed out. Everything about him triggered a reaction in me—desire. Guilt quickly followed.

Since he was with Declan, the town's hockey hero, I can only assume he plays for the Seattle Shooters too. From his physique, his body all strength and power—not that I was really looking, it's just a hard thing *not* to notice when a guy is *that* built—I can only assume he's a defenseman. I'll have to get a hold of Declan's mother, find out who the guy was and send him a box of chocolates as an apology. That almost makes me laugh. I'm soaked because of him and I'm the one apologizing? But seriously, I should have handled the situation better. He's not the reason my phone is gone. Why the heck didn't I listen to the message? I had a whole year. But I already know the answer to that. I couldn't bear to hear Jon's dying words. Maybe in some way that kept him with me, gave me some twisted sort of hope that he wasn't really gone. Unfortunately, that thinking is unhealthy and damaging, and keeps me stuck in the past, yet there is nothing I can, or want, to do about it. Moving onward and forward would be a dishonor to Jon and our marriage.

I hurry up the last steps and push open my apartment door. I'm instantly greeted with a bark and a wagging tail. Miss Mabel, named after Mabel, a lovely lady at Coffee Klatch who took me under her wing when I moved here, is quite happy at the unexpected sight of me. Mabel was the one who suggested a puppy, a chocolate lab, like the name of my shop.

It's like she could see the loss deep inside me, the need for something to love. Mabel had lost her own husband years ago, and if there was one person who knew what I was going through, it was her.

I drop to my knees as Miss Mabel licks at my jacket. "That's yucky, Miss Mabel." I give her a kiss, and stand to check her water bowl, which is almost full. "Would you like to get out for a quick walk before I have to go back to work?" Her tail wags faster and I hurry out of my damp jeans and coat. At least my sweater survived. I tug on yoga pants, a heavy vest, and a different pair of boots as I hang my clothes to dry.

I snatch her leash. "Come on, girl."

Outside she drags me down the sidewalk, wanting to sniff everything. I really need to find the time to get obedience classes. Everyone wants to stop to see the fifty-pound puppy, and she soaks up the attention. As we get closer to Coffee Klatch, she begins to sniff harder, and like a dog on a mission, she makes a beeline for the shop, knowing Mabel will always have a treat for her.

The door opens, and a man steps out, his back to us. Miss Mabel breaks free from me, and I call out to her, but it's too late. The guy turns, something in his hands, and Miss Mabel jumps up on him, knocking him to the wet sidewalk. Mortified, I run and the second I see exactly who she knocked over, the world closes in on me. I've been a good person. I pay my taxes on time. Donate to charities and help my neighbors. Why does life keep throwing me curveballs that knock me on my ass? Or in this case, Mr. Pothole on his ass.

"I'm so sorry," I say and try to drag my big pup off, but the guy is holding her favorite bear claw and she's drooling all over it as he tries to hold it out of her reach.

"Fine, take it," he says and feeds his pastry to her, but at least he's smiling. Correction. He was smiling, until his gaze finds me.

Mabel, my friend, comes rushing outside. Something I don't recognize moves over her face as she takes in the way I can't seem to keep my focus off Mr. Pothole. Wiping her hands on her apron, she says, "Josie Moser, meet Brody Tucker."

"We already met," we both say at the exact same time, and Mabel's grin grows wider. Miss Mabel gobbles the bear claw, and proceeds to lick Brody's hand, and my insides tighten as Brody's gorgeous blue eyes lock on mine. My God, his gaze hits like a warm caress, touching me in all my girly parts—parts that have been dormant for a long time now.

It's wrong to feel this way.

I grab Miss Mabel's leash and tug her off. She turns, sees her namesake and once again goes crazy, jumping up for more goodies. "You've had enough treats," I scold. I turn back to Brody. "I'm so sorry. I'll replace your bear claw, and your clothes. I can wash them or dry clean or whatever."

He sits up, and puts his arms on his knees, like he's in no hurry to move. "That was some great payback."

"It wasn't payback," I explain quickly. I'm not the kind of girl who believes in revenge, and I don't want him, or anyone to think I am. "It was an accident. I promise."

I hold my hand out to help him up, but he refuses it and really, can I blame him? I brace myself, waiting for him to be as ungracious to me as I was to him.

"I got it," he says, pushing to his feet. "You've—"

"Done enough, I know." I swallow down the guilt pushing into my throat as my cheeks heat, undoubtedly turning a bright shade of pink. Seriously though, I deserve everything he's dishing out.

He stands in front of me, and I have to lift my head to see his face. I'm average height, but Mr. Pothole—Brody—is tall. Wide too. Solid. Yeah, I guess if I tried to tug him to his feet, he'd only end up pulling me down on top of his yummy body.

Yummy body?

Good God, who am I? I don't know, but I'm just glad he refused my hand. Falling on him would be horrible, make a rough day even worse, and I am not going to spend one second imagining what it would be like to be on top of him, or underneath him. Nope, not going to spend a millisecond picturing his arms wrapped around me, those big hands on my back, fingers splayed wide, heating me from the inside out as he explores my body. I gulp.

Get it together, girl!

"What I was going to say is, you've been *through* enough already. You know, with me soaking you, earlier."

"It was an accident," I say.

He glances at Miss Mabel. "I won't hold it against her."

"No, I mean—"

Before I can get the words out, apologize again and let him know I realize he didn't soak me on purpose, Declan steps outside. His gaze bobs between the two of us and he backs up an inch, like he just stumbled upon a street fight or something.

"Uh oh." Sweet Miss Mabel jumps up when she sees he's holding a box full of treats. "Whoa."

I grab Mabel at the same time Brody does, and our hands touch, not unexpectedly. But you know what *is* unexpected? The zap of heat that travels through my arm and settles between my legs. I quickly pull my hand back.

"Let me help," Brody says. "She's still a pup and doesn't know her own strength."

He gets hold of Miss Mabel's collar, and kneels on the ground. Since he's already wet, he doesn't need to worry about dampening his knees.

"Hey girl," he says in a low voice that Miss Mabel instantly responds to. "Aren't you pretty." He runs his hand along her head and when he reaches her hindquarters, he gives a push. "Sit, girl." She instantly sits and he smiles up at me. "She's a good girl. She's just excited, and in need of direction."

"What are you, the dog whisperer?" I ask, and even though I'm being very serious, everyone bursts out laughing. Another wave of heat moves into my face, and I'm about to backtrack when Brody turns serious.

"You could say that." He pets Mabel and she sits like a good girl, leaning into him. "I love all animals."

"Miss Mabel seems to love you, too." Mabel says as she glances at me, a new kind of twinkle in her eyes. Good Lord, if she's trying her hand at matchmaking, she can forget it. I am not interested in a relationship with anyone, especially a hockey player who's probably only in town for the holidays. I don't care how good looking he is, or how broad his shoulders are. A guy like him probably knows he's God's gift to women, and no doubt wears it as a badge. I'm just going to do myself a favor and steer clear. "Doesn't she, Josie?"

"What's that?" I ask. Shoot, I'd lost myself in his broad shoulders for a moment...err...I mean I lost my train of thought for a second.

Mabel's grin widens. Dammit, busted. "Miss Mabel seems to love Brody, don't you think?"

Okay, Mabel. Your matchmaking is getting a little blunt here. I adjust my purse on my shoulder and send subliminal messages for her to cut it out. But she continues to smile at me, waiting for an answer. "Uh, yeah sure."

"Hey, she knows a good thing when she sees it," Brody teases, standing, his big body towering over mine.

"Well, she kind of loves everyone, and you were holding her favorite treat."

Declan snorts. "Of course, it was the bear claw," he says, and grins at me. "Did you know Brody had no friends growing up? His parents used to tie a pork chop around his neck just to get the neighborhood dogs to play with him."

"Asshole," Brody says, grinning, grabbing Declan, putting him into a choke hold. I laugh at their antics, tension ebbing from my body as the two play-fight like brothers, and when Mabel grins at me, I straighten my shoulders and pull myself together.

"If you'll excuse me. I'll see about replacing your bear claw. Come on, girl." I take hold of Miss Mabel's leash and tug, but she seems reluctant to leave her new friends.

"Hey," Brody says, letting Declan go. "I'll be in town for the holidays. If you want, I can give Miss Mabel some puppy behavior lessons."

I turn back to him, nibbling my lip. While that does sound good, and I just haven't had a moment to work with her, I can't just hand my pup over to a stranger.

"I...I...well..."

Miss Mabel leans against Brody, in a disgusting display of loyalty, as she wiggles in contentment. I meet her pleading eyes, and suspect she's siding with Mabel, and trying to set me up. Traitors!

Brody's gorgeous blue eyes lock on mine. "I'd love to work with her."

"I can pay you."

"Sure, we can figure out payment later."

He winks at me, and my pulse jumps. Why do I get the feeling that he's not looking for a monetary exchange? My deceitful body takes that moment to heat up, liking the idea. My God, I'm surrounded by traitors! My own body included.

3

BRODY

My mind is on Josie as I pull up to Declan's childhood home, killing the ignition. I take in the twinkling lights on the bushes, as well as the big bulbs hanging from the numerous trees in the yard. An unfamiliar warmth spreads through me, and my chest squeezes.

"People here really love Christmas, huh?" I say, like I find it amusing when the truth is, I kind of like it. But Declan can see right through me, knows me well enough to understand that I had a lot of loss and bury my emotions behind humor. A coping mechanism, I guess.

"It's a thing." From my peripheral vision, I can see the way he's eyeing me, assessing me. I keep staring straight ahead and he opens his door. "Come on."

Grabbing our bags from the trunk, snow crunches beneath my boots as I follow him up the walkway. The front door opens and his mother, a huge inviting smile on her pretty face, spreads her arms when she sees her son coming her way.

As they embrace, my chest aches right around the vicinity of my heart. But I'm not going to let my own lack of family bring me down. Although I have to say, it really would be nice to have a place to call home. I have my house in Boston, decorated by professionals, but it lacks a woman's touch. My thoughts drift to Josie. Everything about her screams home and hearth, and that weird burning sensation in my chest grows as temporary insanity takes hold of my brain, having me imagine what it would be like to rush home to her after a hard day on the ice.

Declan's voice pulls me from my musings as he introduces me to his mother, Donna, and I smile as she pulls me into her arms, like I'm one of her own. I'm about to stop her, not wanting to get her all wet, but she doesn't seem to care, and you know what, it's a nice feeling. A foreign feeling, sure but also a nice one. I'm about to break the hug, but she doesn't let me. Instead she squeezes a little tighter, like she might just know what I'm lacking in my life.

"Brody, welcome." She beams at me as she finally lets me break from the circle of her arms. "We're so happy you're spending the holidays with us."

My heart pounds a little faster, instantly at ease here. "I'm happy to be here," I say, handing over the flowers I purchased for her on Main Street, right after Miss Mabel ate my bear claw.

"Oh how thoughtful." She sniffs the flowers, and her eyes briefly close as she takes pleasure in the floral scent. Her eyes spring back open. "Come in before you catch your death of cold." We step inside and the warmth of the home washes over me, embracing me in a tight squeeze similar to the hug Donna had just given me. "Brody, how did you get all wet?"

Shit. I examine her clothes, note the few wet spots. "I'm sorry if I got—"

She gives me a 'do not worry' wave. "I'm perfectly fine. It's you I'm worried about."

"I slipped."

"Goodness, are you hurt?" My heart does a weird little tumble at her motherly concern.

"Just my pride," I say.

"He was knocked over by a dog looking to get his bear claw," Declan explains, handing the box of donuts over.

Donna laughs. "Let me guess. Miss Mabel."

"The one and only," I say with a laugh.

"She's a delightful little pup, but needs a bit of training. Josie is so busy with the shop, but the pup has been good company for her." She goes quiet for a second, and it's followed by a frown and then a tsking sound. "All alone in that loft over the shop. That's just not right."

"She's new here?" Declan asks. "I don't remember seeing her around."

"Moved here from Boston last year. Lovely girl. She owns the chocolate shop on Main." Donna folds her hands together and a dreamy look comes over her face. "She has the best chocolate nips."

I nearly swallow my tongue. "Ah, what?" I ask, my mind taking a trip down the 'inappropriate thoughts' lane.

Donna makes a little square with her fingers. "These amazing little chocolate nips, with caramel in the middle. Delicious. You'll have to try them." I do my best not to look at Declan, because he'll be smirking—his thoughts as wrong as mine—and I don't want to burst out laughing, and have to explain why.

"I'm sure Brody would love to try her nips," Declan says, almost under his breath, and I bite the inside of my cheek to keep my shit together. As soon as I get him alone, I'm going to give him a beat down.

Donna smiles at me. "Now why don't you run upstairs and change, and we'll have coffee and donuts." Declan's phone pings, and he pulls it from his pocket. A smile spreads across his face as he quickly texts back.

Donna shakes her head at me. "Must be Nikki. He always smiles like that when it's Nikki."

I nod, and resist the urge to ask what the story is between the two when Donna says, "She'll be joining us for Christmas Eve dinner." She claps her hands together, delight all over her face. It's easy to tell how much she likes Nikki from her reaction. "You'll be joining us too, won't you?"

I inject enthusiasm into my voice when I say, "Yeah, sure. Sounds like fun." I mean, it's not that I'm not looking forward to it, it's the whole thing about having to bring a date. This week is about downtime, and I'm just so damn played out. While the idea of spending time with Josie doesn't seem like a hardship, I have my work cut out for me there.

"You'll be bringing someone, won't you? If not, Declan's cousin—"

I hold my hands up to cut her off. "I'll be bringing someone."

"Someone I know?" she asks with a raised brow. "Someone local, perhaps?"

"Someone local." I can tell she's about to ask who, so I tug at my wet clothes. "I should get out of these."

"Right." She points to the wide staircase, "Second door on the right." She smells her flowers again. "I must get these in some water."

"Thanks, Donna." I grab my bag and head up as Declan loses himself in his phone. I undress and pull clean clothes from my bag. I climb into them and drop down onto the bed, stretching out my legs as I pull the shiny object I found in the snowbank from my pocket.

I honestly have no idea if I'll be able to open Josie's phone. Most people have passcodes. I slide my finger over the screen and it lights up. Son of a bitch. I lay there for a moment, and a measure of guilt starts in my gut and spreads out. She seemed pretty bummed that she lost her phone, and I'm an honest guy, so by rights, I should give it back. Opening it is an invasion of her privacy and I am so not that type of guy. Hell, I wouldn't want anyone doing that to me.

As an NHL player, my life is always being photographed, my every move scrutinized. I realize how important privacy is. But when I spotted the phone, and with Declan egging me on, I made a stupid impulsive decision to keep it. Now that I'm going to work with her dog, I don't really need to peek into her life, to find an easy way for me to insert myself into it. Of course, that doesn't mean I would have went ahead and looked at her pictures if fate hadn't dealt a different hand.

I set the phone down, guilt swelling inside me. I'm going to have to give it back, but how can I do that now? She probably thinks the plow carried it away and today, everything is stored on the cloud, so it's not like she's going to lose anything important, right? If I give it to her now, she'll know I took it, and there goes any chance of getting a Christmas Eve date, or spending time with her. Because when it comes right down to it, there was a lot about her that intrigued me. Maybe we could hang out over Christmas, have some fun, and to make up for what it's going to cost to replace her old phone, I can buy a shit ton of chocolate and have it shipped to friends and family back in Boston.

Feeling a little better about the whole situation, I tuck her phone into my bag, pull my own out and do a search on Josie before I step into the hall. I don't find much on social media and I'm about to do a little deeper digging when a booming male voice reaches my ears, followed by laughter, and I can only guess Declan's father is home. I make my way to the kitchen to find Declan, as well as his mom and dad, sitting around the table like a happy family. I go still, about to back up. The image before me is a happy one, picture perfect, and I do not want to intrude upon family time.

"Brody, son, get in here," Declan's father says. He stands, taking my hand in his, shaking it as he pulls me in for a big bear of a hug. I'm tall, yet I still have to glance up to meet the man's eyes.

"Mr. Bradbury, so nice to meet you."

"Call me Fred, son."

Every time he calls me son, my heart squeezes a little tighter and I don't miss the way Declan is watching me, checking in on me. He's a good friend, always worried about me. I love that about him. I give him a slight nod to let him know I'm good.

"Nice to meet you, Fred."

He claps my shoulder. "That's better. Now come on, join us for coffee and tell me more about yourself." He laughs. "I can't believe you're the son of the infamous Carl Tucker. It must have been great growing up with him as your role model."

I nod, and even though growing up with Carl Tucker was anything but pleasant, I keep a few stories on hand for times like these. It's not like there weren't good times. There were, they were just few and far between. But he's a beloved hockey star and I'm not going to take that away from him or darken his reputation.

I sit and Declan gives me a nod, understanding what I'm going through and for the next couple of hours, we talk. I have to say, Declan's family is warm, loving and quick to take me under their wing, and I'm grateful that they're not asking why I'm spending Christmas with them instead of my own family.

After hours of catching up, Declan glances around the table. "I'm going to take off for a few hours. You good here?"

"Actually, I thought I'd head down Main Street, get some last-minute shopping done."

"Dad, can I borrow your car?" Declan asks and his father laughs. He pulls the keys from his pocket, tossing them across the table.

He shakes his head but it's easy to tell how much he loves having Declan home—borrowing his car like old times. "Some things never change."

Leaving the table, I tug on my winter coat. "I can drop you."

"Nah, you go do your thing. I'll catch up with you later. Hallmark movie and beer," he says, winking as he claps my back.

"You're such an asshole."

"An asshole who's got your back."

"And vice versa." I glance back over my shoulder catching his parents in an embrace in the kitchen. There is no doubt Declan is loved by all, but it's best I don't let that go to his head. "Are you going to see Nikki?"

"Yeah."

"Speaking of having your back. If you want to talk—"

"Nothing to talk about. Seriously. Nothing. We're just friends." His head hangs a bit, like he's clearly upset about that, and walks out the door, putting an end to the conversation.

Ten minutes later, I'm cruising down Main Street and the place is lit up like...well, like a Christmas tree. It's so damn quaint, it could be a picture straight out of a Norman Rockwell photo. I like it. A lot. I slow my car down outside The Chocolate Lab and a laugh bubbles up inside me as I put two and two together. Josie has a chocolate lab named Miss Mabel. Of course, she does. I park on the street, and step from the vehicle, being careful to avoid any surprise potholes.

I pull open the door to the chocolate shop and I'm hit with delicious smells, but my mind instantly goes to Josie's nips, or rather nipples, when I spot her talking quite intently to a customer. Her gaze flitters to mine, and for a second, I spot something there. Something so uneasy and jittery it makes me want to jump to her rescue. Is the guy giving her a hard time, or something? She looks back at the man who appears to be in his early forties, with premature graying hair.

Before I even realize what I'm doing, I walk toward them, my steps determined, and a wide smile spreads across Josie's face as I approach. I'm about to intervene, when a laugh bubbles in her throat and she throws her arms around me, nearly knocking me on my ass, much the same way her dog did earlier.

"Please just go with it," she whispers into my ear. Her arms slide around my back, and I put mine around her tiny body, anchoring her to me and showing possession, because yeah, I guess I am man enough to admit I watch Hallmark movies, so I sort of get what she's going for here.

"I'm so happy to see you," she squeals and breaks from the circle of my arms. "I was just telling Patrick you were running late, and that you might not even be able to make it at all with your demanding schedule."

"Nothing short of a hurricane blowing me off the road could keep me from you, sweetness," I say, sliding my arm around her waist, pulling her back to me. Her body collides with mine and I don't miss the shiver that moves through her.

"Honey, I'd like you to meet Patrick. He's our local sheriff and a loyal customer."

I extend my arm taking his hand in mine. "Of course, he is. You do make the best chocolate in all of Massachusetts."

Patrick doesn't laugh. Heck, he doesn't even smile. He just stands there staring at me in that inquisitive way cops do, and I can't tell if it's because I'm a NHL player or he's thinking about ways to arrest me, because he's clearly into Josie, and I'm the guy standing in as her pretend boyfriend because she's not into him. I let go of his hand.

"You're...you're Brody Tucker."

"You're a fan of the Shooters?" I ask.

"Yes, I've known Declan for years." He grins at Josie, his shoulders relaxing slightly. "I can't believe you never told me you were dating Brody Tucker."

She opens and closes her mouth, and I come to her rescue. "I like to keep my private life private, you know?"

"Yes, of course, I totally understand that." Patrick shakes his head, a smile tugging at his mouth. "How did you two meet?"

Josie goes pale, and I jump in and say, "Oh, let's just say it was fate that brought us together. It's going to be a great story for the grandkids. Isn't that right, sweetness?"

"You two are very serious, then," he whispers, almost to himself as he takes a small step back. "I'd love to get your autograph later. You've been on the road with the team, and I'm sure you two lovebirds probably want to be alone."

"You're right. Alone time with my lovebird is definitely a priority and I'd be happy to sign something for you next time."

I lean in, kissing Josie on the cheek, and heat crawls up her neck, coloring her skin pink. I'm being a smart ass, but I can't help myself. She's so adorable when she's flustered, and she can't knee me in the nuts with Patrick watching us, thinking we're a couple—and hey, this is on her. She initiated it. I'm just playing the part. I'm sure it will be a different story when he leaves, but right now, I'm just going to have some fun with it. Not only that. Since I'm doing her this favor, I could probably turn this around and ask her to do me one and go to Christmas Eve dinner, but you know what, I don't want to do that. I don't want her to feel obligated to help me. I'd rather she come if she wants to come, not because she feels indebted.

"I've missed my little lovebird so much." I lift her clear off the ground, and she makes a wheezing sound as I spin her around.

Patrick laughs and Josie joins in, but the sound is strained, and the look in her eyes is anything but amused.

Dear nuts...I am so sorry about the knee you are about to receive.

"What a lovely couple you two make. It's easy to see how much you two love each other." He nods to me. "Well, I'll be on my way."

"See you later, Patrick." I grin at him. "Don't come by too early tomorrow. My little chocolatier might be late for work. We have some catching up to do. If you know what I mean?"

Patrick chuckles as he exits the store and Josie turns to me, her eyes shooting daggers, as one hand goes to her face, her fingers lingering on the spot I kissed. "What the hell do you think you're doing?"

I grin at her. "That was my first question. My second is what kind of perks come with this fake relationship?"

4

JOSIE

"No, it's not like that. Wait...I mean..."

"Hey, it's okay," he says. "I'm just kidding. I do that sometimes." I stare at him and he cocks his head. "You know what joking is, right?"

He's grinning at me but it's not lightening my mood. "And... what do you mean fate brought us together? In what universe does fate spray someone with slush?"

"This one, and it's called a meet cute."

Okay, I do love a good meet cute, but this was anything but. "My life isn't a romantic comedy and there was nothing cute about nearly freezing to death." My God, I sound like a crazy woman. I already established that it wasn't his fault. He didn't do it on purpose. The reason I'm lashing out is I like the idea of perks, and I really shouldn't be making a mental list.

He holds his hands up, palms out. "Sorry, I just happened to believe everything happens for a reason."

"It's going to take a whole lot of eggnog and maybe a Christmas miracle to convince me of that, Brody."

"Think about it, you just happened to be on the street. I just happened to be driving by when Declan yelled at me to pull over."

"I didn't just happen to be on the street. I lost my phone and was looking for it."

Something comes over his face, something that looks like guilt, and I take a breath. "Sorry, I realize it wasn't your fault. I was just upset about losing my phone."

"Can you replace it?"

"Yeah," I say, not bothering to tell him there are things on my phone that aren't replaceable. He doesn't need to know my problems.

"And again now." He waves around the shop. "I happened to be here at the right time to help you out with a little problem. That, my friend, is fate."

"Fate, huh?"

"Yeah."

"You believe what's going to happen is going to happen." He nods. "Let me ask you a question, then. Do you look both ways before you cross the street?"

His eyes narrow, and he stares at me long and hard. Something flickers in his eyes, a light bulb going off and a laugh rumbles in his chest, and I can't help but grin. "All right. You've got me there."

"I mean, why not just walk right out? If you were meant to get hit by a car, you would have gotten hit, right?"

He holds his hands up. "Okay, I get it." He gestures with a nod toward the door. "What was that all about anyway?"

I usually like to keep my private life private, although in this small town, rumors spread like wildfire and I'm sure everyone knows I'm a widow, even though no one brings it up and the only one I ever shared my tragic past with was Mabel. Under the circumstances, however, I do owe Brody an explanation.

I put my hands over my eyes groaning, trying to figure out a way to word it. The next thing I know his warm hands are on mine, and holy God, the streak of warmth careening through my blood from a simple touch is absolutely lightning-strike insane. What is it about this guy that gets me all fired up without even trying? I've not been attracted to anyone since Jon. Haven't wanted to be attracted to anyone, and this hockey player comes sauntering into town like he owns it, and without even trying, messes with my carefully constructed life.

I should run, get out now.

Oh, but he's your pretend boyfriend now, Josie.

Dammit.

He tugs my hands from my face. "You don't have to tell me if you don't want to."

"That was Patrick," I say with a heavy sigh. "He's such a nice man, so sweet and a huge supporter of my business. He's the first customer every morning and the last customer every night."

"He sounds terrible." He scrunches up his face like he just tasted something nasty. "I would have pretended to be in a relationship to get rid of him too. Good call."

I glare at him, and do my best not to laugh at his antics. He is kind of funny. "It's not like that."

"I'm kidding. You know that." He twists his lips. "But I can only guess it's not just your chocolate he likes."

"I guess. He's asked me out a few times. Or a dozen."

"And that's not something you want?"

"I don't date." I blurt that out so fast and with such conviction, his brow arches and before he can ask me why, I continue. "I hate to hurt anyone's feelings so I..."

"Wait," He says and holds his hands up. "You had no trouble hurting my feelings this afternoon. I'm pretty sure you told me to go get driving lessons."

I cringe, covering my face again. "I'm sorry. I was upset. I shouldn't have taken it out on you. Please, tell me how I can make that up to you."

"Hey," he says his voice soft and soothing as he takes my hand, this time holding it between his, and I work extra hard not to melt at his feet as his warmth seeps into my skin. I glance down, note the way his big palm smothers my small hand. Oddly enough, it doesn't make me feel small, but instead fills me with a sense of security and comfort, and I haven't felt that way in a long time. In fact, I've been taking care of myself, been alone since...since my late husband. "I'm just kidding." He gives me a wink. "I'm tougher than that. You should hear what the guys say to me when I'm off my game and the opposing team gets a breakaway."

"I doubt that ever happens. Look at you." I gaze at his rough and tough physique, admire the small scar on his face. It gives him character, adds to his charm.

Stop thinking about him like that, Josie.

"What's that supposed to mean?"

In an exaggerated manner, I blow out a breath. "You're not just a smart ass, you're a smart guy. You know what I mean."

"I'm sure there was a compliment buried in there somewhere." We both laugh, tension easing from my body as he lifts himself up to his full height, clearly liking the way I admire his strength and stature.

"Look, I really am sorry." I think about losing my phone, the last message left to me by my late husband. It's strange really. I used to think everything happened for a reason, too, but I can't see the reason behind my phone being carried away by a plow. "Have you ever had a bad day, and wondered what you did in a past life to deserve it?"

"All the time," he says in a soft, supportive voice that commiserates with me, and it's weird, but I like that he understands, that he's on my side. His head lifts and he looks past my shoulders when we hear a noise out back. I turn, and through the glass partition that allows customers to watch us make chocolate, I spot Kayley putting things away for the night.

"That's Kayley. She's my assistant and I must warn you, she's a big fan. Despite your reputation."

He grins as I not so subtly let him know I'm aware of his game—his off-ice game that is. "Which means you obviously brought me up to her."

"I had no choice but to mention the slush incident. I came in here soaking wet and nearly frozen to death."

"So you did bring me up?"

I shake my head at him. "That's your takeaway?"

"That, and you clearly couldn't stop thinking about me, then?"

His grin turns playful, maybe even a bit cocky, and it teases all my girly parts. Kayley was right. This guy is a player, on and off the ice, and I'd be wise to remember that. "I told her you splashed me, and that Miss Mabel knocked you to the ground and ate your bear claw." What I didn't tell her was that Brody Tucker was the hottest guy on the face of the earth, and he damn well knows it, and I damn well like it.

"Hi Kayley," he says, acknowledging my assistant as she comes from the back, which is kind of nice. But I guess he's a guy who knows how to keep his fans happy. They do, after all, pay his salary, so to speak. I turn to see Kayley go still, her jaw practically on the counter.

"Hi," she squeaks out. "You know my name."

Miss Mabel barks from upstairs, like she knows Brody is in the house and she wants her time with him too.

"Josie told me."

"Get over here," I say, and Kayley takes off her apron, smooths her hand over her hair, and steps up to us. She extends her hand and Brody shakes it. My God, my assistant is practically vibrating, not to mention drooling, but I get it. Brody has that effect on people, and I'm no exception. Kayley pulls her phone out.

"Do you mind?"

"Not at all." He takes her phone, and looks at me. "Do you want to make it a threesome?" He shakes his head and laughs. "I mean..."

"I know what you mean and no, I'm good. Thanks." I stand back as Brody takes a selfie of the two of them. Kayley is a giggling mess as she walks back to the counter and puts her coat on.

"We're just closing up," I tell him. "Were you here to get something?" He grins at me, and that's when I realize the mistake in my words. "I mean, do you want some chocolate?"

"I know what you mean," he says, and I hate that my cheeks are warming, a dead giveaway that I'm thinking about sex. From his threesome comment and the way he quickly corrected himself, I'm not the only one entertaining inappropriate thoughts here.

"See you later," Kayley says, the bell jingling as she leaves the store, and now, with the two of us standing there, a little nervous quiver moves through me. I search my brain for something to say. My God, I'm usually a great conversationalist, but now I'm tongue-tied. Upstairs, Miss Mabel continues to bark, and it seems to break some of the tension arcing between us. My brain finally kicks into gear.

"Oh, are you here for Mabel?" I ask.

"Actually no, I came to see you."

He rocks toward me and I'm suddenly aware of the little nervous quiver in my stomach. I search my brain for something to say.

"What did you need, Brody?" My body warms all over, thinking about what I want...what I need. I haven't had this kind of attention from a hot guy in...well since I lost my husband. At that reminder, I straighten my shoulders and quickly pull myself together. Brody angles his head, like he can sense the change in me.

"I wanted to make sure you were okay."

"I'm okay," I say. It's a lie. I've not been okay in a long time. "Thanks again for helping me out with Patrick."

"You know there's a big problem, right?" I shake my head, having no idea what he's talking about. He points a finger back and forth between the two of us. "If we're supposed to be a couple, isn't Patrick going to be wondering why I'm staying with Declan and not you?"

Blood drains to my toes. Ohmigod, he's right. I panicked earlier, never thought through the logistics of a fake relationship. Or maybe I did. Maybe on some level, this is what I wanted. God, what has this man done to me?

"I can stay with Declan, although I'm sure he's going to be spending the bulk of his time between his family and Nikki. His place is really nice, and his folks are great, but we're adults, Josie. Adults do adult things. Don't you think Patrick is going to think our sleeping situations are a little off?"

"I'm not sleeping with you," I blurt out, and the second I do, my traitorous brain takes me down a titillating path where I play out that idea. Brody in my bed. On top of me. His big bear-like hands on my body, awakening things in me that have been dormant for a long time.

"I'm not asking you to."

His eyes are full of warm sincerity as his gaze moves over my face. Please God, do not give him the ability to read me. I do not want him privy to my secret thoughts, because there is no way I'm sleeping with him, and I don't want him thinking he has a shot. Yeah, sure my body is saying something entirely different, but I can't. I won't.

I give a curt nod. "Good."

"I'm just pointing out the obvious," he says, and I blink up at him, waiting to hear more. "I'll help you out, whatever you want." I stare at him, hearing nothing but sincerity in his voice. Truthfully, I'm not sensing an ulterior motive here. The guy that sleeps around might not be looking to get into my bed, and I really have no idea why disappointment is careening through my blood, turning me into a sulking teenage girl.

What the hell is wrong with me?

Oh, maybe it's because it's been too long since you've felt desired, and this guy wants to sleep with everyone but you.

As that truth settles like a stone in my gut—as ridiculous as that is—I take a small step back, giving myself a reprieve from the clean soapy scent of his skin, not to mention the heat emanating from him and warming my coldest corners.

"...so what do you say, want to go free her?"

"What?" I ask, so lost in my thoughts I'm not exactly sure what he's asking. All I know is he said something about freeing her. Does that mean he can read me, realize that my body is aching to break free with this man?

"Miss Mabel. She's barking nonstop. Want to free her and take her for a walk?"

"Oh, yeah sure." I step around him, lock the door, and turn the sign to closed. "I'll be right back."

"Or I could come up. I suppose I should know what your place is like. You know, since you're my girl and all."

My girl.

A fine quiver goes through me as that thought rattles around in my brain. "Yeah, you're right. I don't know where my brain is lately."

Sure you do, Josie. It's centered between your legs at the moment.

"Follow me," I say. I walk to the back room, and it's only when I'm on the second step that I realize Brody isn't behind me. I turn back, and smile as his eyes go wide.

"Wait, you actually make chocolate here? Like *make it* make it? From beans?"

"That's what a chocolatier does."

"The chocolate lab." He slaps his palm to his forehead and I wonder if he's always this dramatic. I kind of like his zest, to be honest. "I get it now. I guess I just thought you bought chocolate and sold it."

"Nope, I actually make chocolate from ethically sourced cacao beans."

His eyes glisten, with respect. "You're like a chemist." My chest swells, appreciating his admiration of my craft.

"Sort of."

"Where did you learn all this?"

"My parents. They came here from Switzerland when I was just a baby. They had their own shop, and I took it over after they..." I take a breath as my heart pinches. I miss my folks, my family back in Switzerland.

His knuckles brush mine, the simple, barely there touch sending sparks through my body. "I'm sorry, Josie. I didn't mean to bring up hard memories."

"No, no," I say quickly. "They're still alive. They moved back to Switzerland when my Dad's mother got sick. My life was in Boston, so I stayed."

"You haven't been in Holiday Peak long?"

"No, not that long."

His look is full of playful indignation when he says, "Yet you had the nerve to call me an out of towner."

I laugh at his teasing, which he does a lot. "Like I said, I'll make up for being grouchy somehow. But this town. It was my favorite place to visit when I lived in Boston. My favorite place to shop, especially at Christmas." I go quiet for a second, remembering all the fun Jon and I had visiting during the holidays, all the craft markets and winter activities. The memories warm me and make me sad at the same time. "Holiday Peak kind of sucks you in, and in no time at all, you feel like you've always belonged." It's no wonder I moved here last year and relocated my chocolate shop shortly after.

He nods, and looks down, like his thoughts are a million miles away. "I walked into Declan's house, and his folks took me right in, like I was one of their own."

"You get it then."

He nods, an almost sad, melancholy look briefly crosses his eyes. I'm about to ask him why he's here with Declan and not with his own family, when Miss Mabel barks again.

He snaps out of whatever trance he'd been in and smiles. "We'd better get her out."

"You're right." I hurry up the stairs and he follows behind. I open the door, and Mabel pushes past me and nearly knocks Brody down the stairs. "Why hello to you too," I say, and after Brody gives her a good amount of love, she comes running back to me. "Everyone's a traitor."

"What's that?"

"Nothing. Come on in. Let me feed her, and then we'll take her out." I get her food from the pantry, dumping it into her bowl. She's a food-driven dog, but apparently, she likes Brody more than her kibble. I stand there with my hands on my hips as he drops down to the floor with my oversized pup, and I can't help but smile as he plays with her. Mabel nips and yelps, her tail going a million miles an hour. I had no idea how much she's been craving male attention until now.

Lord, I had no idea how much *I've* been craving male attention, not until Brody. Not that I'm going to do anything about that. Brody's deep laughter curls around me as Mabel goes down on her front paws, totally in play mode. My heart misses a beat, loving the scene playing out before me.

I lean against the counter, taking it all in. I'm not sure why I like seeing Brody in my place so much, or like the way he seems to fit so easily. Maybe because no man has ever entered my home, and it's been lacking a male presence. Not to mention Miss Mabel's instant comradery with him. She likes all people, but she's certainly attaching herself to Brody in a big way. Animals can sense when someone truly loves them and from the way she's going berserk, I'm guessing Brody— despite his reputation—really is one of the good guys. Mabel is a good judge of character like that.

For a brief, ridiculous moment, I let my thoughts drift. What would it be like if Brody really was my boyfriend, home for the holidays to be with me? Naturally he'd be staying with me, sleeping in my bed. While we don't have to go that far, maybe he could stay here. He'd have his privacy all day long while I was at work, and he'd be great company for Mabel, not to mention he wants to help with her training. Then again, would he even want to stay? He's home with his buddy. Maybe they want quiet bonding time or something.

Ask him.

"I'm wondering if...maybe you should hang out here, you know...spend the night or two. You were right when you pointed out that if we were a real couple, you'd be staying here." I laugh, but it sounds nervous and unsure. "Won't that give the townsfolk something to gossip about?"

Careful, Josie. Are you doing this for the ruse, or because you like being around this guy?

He pushes to his feet giving Mabel a head rub. "Get your dinner, girl." Mabel trots off to her bowl, her tail still wagging. Brody's head lifts and when those gorgeous blue eyes meet mine, I realize I've made a mistake. I shouldn't have asked. I shouldn't have brought it up. He's temptation with a capital T, and I just can't...

"Before we go any further, we need to talk about the rules of this relationship," he says, a teasing glimmer in his eyes.

I fold my arms, not because I'm upset with his teasing, or that he might actually want more, but to hide the hardening of my nipples. "You mean the perks?"

His grin is wildly playful, and pure seduction. "Just so you know, if I do stay to help you with this ruse, that doesn't mean I'm putting out."

5

BRODY

Five days until Christmas Eve:

Josie was right. I am a smart ass. I can only imagine what a therapist would say about that. But maybe it's true. Maybe I do hide my deficiencies behind humor. The fact is, deep down I want—crave—what my buddies are finding. A wife, kids, the damn minivan and dog. I just don't have what it takes to make a woman want to stay, and I don't play with hearts, which is why I make it perfectly clear to all, right from the beginning, that I have a rotating bedroom door. Josie said she knew about my reputation, and that's good. She should know who's sleeping in her spare room.

As I lay in her bed—in her spare bedroom—I toss restlessly, the early morning sun rising on the horizon and casting shadows on the wall. A wave of peaceful contentment moves through me. Perhaps it has something to do with her comfortable bed. I don't want to move. When was the last time I felt like this? I'm not sure, and I'm not sure what it is about her place that feels like home, despite the fact that it's sparsely decorated, and she doesn't even have a tree up. I plan to rectify that.

I actually can't believe she asked me to stay. I wasn't joking when I said it would look odd if I slept at Declan's place and not my 'girlfriend's.' She found herself in a sticky situation trying not to hurt someone's feelings and while that's commendable—she's sweeter than the chocolate she makes— the two of us are now forced to spend time together. While I don't have a problem with that, I can't help but think honesty is the best policy.

Then why didn't you tell her you have her phone?

I already know the answer to that, and I want to hang out with her. Maybe that has more to do with the fact that I like being around her than in needing a damn dinner date. I've never really felt such a fast connection with a woman, not that I think this is going anywhere. I leave after the holidays and she's not the man-hater I thought she was. In fact, she's far too sweet for me.

Maybe she's not the kind of woman who would leave?

Who am I kidding? I eventually screw everything up, which means the two of us can only be friends and I need to stop cracking sexual jokes. The sound of Mabel's bone-shaped nametag jingling on her collar reaches my ears, and I kick my blankets off, ready to take her out for a morning run, when down the hall a door opens and closes.

I tug on my jeans and sweater to investigate, and check my phone for messages. I texted Declan last night to let him know I'd be staying at Josie's, and of course, he took it the wrong way, thinking I'm sleeping with the woman who wanted to neuter me earlier in the day. But why wouldn't he think that? It's my M.O. and everyone knows it. I didn't bother correcting him, but I do wonder how he made out with Nikki. He's always so secretive about her.

The sound of children playing in the distance fills the silence of Josie's loft, and I pad to the window to see a big snow hill covered with kids squealing and laughing as they slide down. I spot Josie walking Mabel, and the kids running up to her to pat the big puppy. Mabel jumps all over them, and while that's cute now, when she's a full-grown dog, it can pose a danger. No worries, I know how to work with her.

I make my way to the kitchen, glancing around her loft. Why doesn't she have any personal pictures on her walls? There are art pieces, but no family photos, nothing to say she comes from a loving home. In the kitchen, I pour a cup of coffee, thankful that she'd made a carafe as I root through the fridge. I find all the ingredients to make breakfast, but first, a shower.

I take my time lathering up, since Josie isn't back yet, and once I'm clean, I dress, and head back to the kitchen to get straight to work. After I put the bacon in the pan, I grab my phone and do a search, a plan forming in the back of my brain. When I find what I want, I tuck my phone away and I'm just putting the toast down, wondering what's taking her so long, when the door opens and in walks Josie, her cheeks a pretty shade of pink from the cold. My heart squeezes. God, she's adorable.

Why again is it she can't be mine?

Right, right, I mess everything up.

"What are you doing?" she asks, as Mabel comes barreling at me like a damn bowling ball. "Hey girl, sit," I say, and put pressure on her hind end to get her to sit. She listens, and I drop down to give her praise as Josie stands there watching. I glance up at her.

"In Boston, we call this breakfast," I tease.

She rolls her eyes at me. "I know but you're cooking…"

I stand. "I'm a man of many talents." She steps up to the counter and pours a mug of coffee. Her stomach takes that moment to growl, and I laugh. "You can't live on chocolate alone, you know."

"You're a hockey player. I just assumed you had a cook or something." She takes a sip of coffee. "This is really nice, Brody. Thank you."

My heart crashes against my chest as her gratitude warms my blood, making me want to do more, everything for her. I finally find my voice and say, "Have a seat, m'lady."

She laughs, and drops down into a chair. I place her food in front of her and she's about to jump up, but I stop her.

"I got it," I say and pull utensils from the drawer.

"Wow, a girl could get used to this."

"Every good boyfriend should make his girl breakfast, especially a girl who runs her own business, and has a pup who runs her off her feet, don't you think?" Her brow arches, like she's surprised by my observation. "What?" I ask.

"Nothing." She tosses a piece of bacon into her mouth. "This is just really nice. It's been a long time since…" She lets her words fall off and I don't push.

"What are your plans for the day?" I ask. It's Saturday, and I assume she's busy with the shop, but that doesn't mean she can't take a break and do something fun, or maybe I could help her out downstairs. I don't know anything about chocolate, but I'm a fast learner.

"Work, it's crazy this time of year."

I want to ask about a tree, but I'm not sure how to broach the subject. I know firsthand Christmas isn't a wonderful time of year for everyone.

"Something on your mind?" she asks as Mabel comes up and plunks herself down next to me.

I laugh and before I ask her about not having a tree, I point to Mabel. "Know what this is called?" She glances at Mabel and back at me, her brow furrowed. "It's called POF," I say, and a deeper confusion moves over her face. I grab a slice of bacon and feed it to Mabel. "She sits where there is POF, probability of food."

Josie laughs, and the sound fills the kitchen and my soul with lightness. Man, I really like when she laughs, and something tells me she doesn't do it often enough.

"And to answer your question, I do have something on my mind." She takes a sip of coffee and stares at me over the rim, waiting for me to continue. "You don't have a tree."

Her face pales a little and she sets the cup down and my insides clench. Shit, I clearly hit a sore spot and didn't mean to upset her. As she goes quiet, lost in thought, I turn this around, making it about me, talking about something private, something I don't usually share.

"When I was growing up, there were times we never had a tree."

Her brow bunches. "Really? I'm sorry, Brody."

"Dad was on the road a lot, and well I had many..." I stop and do air quotes around the word, "Moms." Her face softens and catching me off guard, she reaches across the table and takes my hand into hers.

"That must have been hard."

I shrug, brushing it off, but I'm pretty sure she can see right through that. "I don't usually do Christmas in a big way. In fact, I usually do it alone, but I usually put a tree up."

She nods. "I guess if you're going to be staying here, we need a tree then huh?"

"Are you okay with that?"

She glances down, and her face is tight, her thoughts a million miles away. What kind of demon is she fighting? The impulse to jump in and fight it for her overcomes me. I might not be her boyfriend, but that doesn't mean I can't be her friend. I'm about to tell her to forget it, that we don't need a tree if it'll upset her, when her head lifts, a small smile on her face.

"I'm okay with that."

Warmth and happiness move through me. "I did a little research earlier."

Her brow arches, and her curious smile makes me laugh. "Do I have to guess what this research was?"

"I was going to tell you, but since you're being a smart-ass, now I won't. I'll just surprise you instead."

"I don't really like surprises, Brody," she says and pulls a new phone from her pocket.

Guilt niggles at me. "You replaced your phone?"

"Yes, this morning, after Mabel and I had a walk."

She checks the time. "I'm running late. I don't usually sit down to a nice breakfast before rushing off to work." She stands and takes her dish to the sink.

"Go down." I give her a wink. "Although you might want to stall for a bit to drive the point home to Patrick that we celebrated last night in a big way."

She blushes. "I don't think that's necessary." She starts to do the dishes and I step up to her, put my hands on her hips and move her aside.

"I got this and afterward, Miss Mabel and I are going to do some training, aren't we Mabel?" Her tail wags so hard, it thumps on the leg of the table.

"She really likes you."

"What's not to like?" I tease.

Without a pause, she says, "I could make a list, but I don't want to be late for work." She goes quiet, thoughtful, then adds, "I heard you had that effect on girls, and little Miss Mabel here is not immune to the sweet talker."

"I'm the sweet talker and you're the sweet maker. What a team, huh? Also, how do you know that about me? Creeping my Instagram?" Yeah, okay, I creeped hers, but didn't find anything personal, which is a bit weird. She mostly puts pictures up of her business.

She gives a quick shake of her head. "No, Kayley filled me in, and honestly, Brody, I don't care if you sleep around. I'm not judging you. I'm just not into that."

"I know. I'm not looking for that from you, remember?"

She smiles but it doesn't reach her eyes. "Yeah, I remember."

Okay, if she's so happy about that, why the heck is her brow furrowed, a deep disappointment swimming in her big brown eyes, like I just kicked her pup or something? Does she want me to want sex from her, even though she keeps driving home the point that she's not sleeping with me?

"Maybe that's a tiny lie," I say, gauging her reaction. "You're a beautiful woman, Josie and I'd sleep with you if you twisted my arm…or even my finger, maybe even a hair on my finger."

A smile lights up her face, but she quickly hides it. "You have hair on your fingers?"

I laugh and look at my hands. "I think I do. Don't you?"

She laughs hard and I love this lightness about her. "Don't worry. I'm not about to twist anything."

Goddammit, now there are things I really want to twist.

"I never said I was worried. Wait, what was that you said about a list?" She laughs, and I love her quick wit. "You're kind of a smart ass too, aren't you?"

"I think you're rubbing off on me." Her eyes open wide, and I can't help but think the word rubbing is messing with her, in much the same way it's messing with me. "I mean…"

"I know what you mean, now go. I have plans for us later, so don't work too late."

She hesitates for a moment, and I sense she wants to tell me something but instead she bends to pet Mabel.

"You be a good girl."

Two minutes later, I'm alone with sweet Mabel, and I refill her water bowl and wash up the dishes. "Okay girl, you ready to go play?"

She jumps up and I tug on my coat and ballcap and leash her. A few minutes later, we're walking through town, and I check out all the stores as tourists who are here for a skiing holiday fill the streets. Miss Mabel is a big old chick magnet and we're stopped a hundred times before we can make it to the park. Everyone wants to pet the pup, and even with my ballcap pulled low, most people recognize me, which means a ton of selfies. Not that I mind. What I do mind, however, is all the numbers that are slipped into my pocket. I'm not sure why that's suddenly bothering me when it never has in the past.

I finally get Mabel to the park, and we spend the next hour or so working on commands, especially call back, sit, stay and heel. She's going to need to learn to walk properly before she's full grown, otherwise she's going to drag Josie down the street on her rear end. I smile, not at the image of Josie getting dragged by her dog, but because I like thinking of her. I liked seeing her smile this morning, and while her past is her past, I can't help but want to know more about her. What really brought her here, why does she hate surprises and what's the real reason behind not putting up a tree in a town that takes Christmas to the extreme? If she hated the holiday so much, surely she wouldn't have move to a town with the name holiday in it, right?

I walk Mabel home and hurry downstairs. I'm anxious to see Josie, not just because I want to tell her about Mabel's progress, but...dammit, I just want to see her. I find her in the back, dressed in her jeans and a dark T-shirt, covered by a black apron that dips below her knees. Her hair is pulled back and tucked inside a net, and it's ridiculous how cute she looks. I grin as I walk toward her, not wanting to disturb her deep concentration, but I am curious about that strange tug on my chest as I close the distance. She smiles when I approach, and the way it lights up her face pulls at me. It's all I can do to remember we're only friends. If we weren't, I'd drag her into my arms, and this time, kiss her on the mouth.

I touch her cheek, brush the chocolate away, and bring it to my mouth for a taste, although I really wish I hadn't. That sweet taste teases of something more, something I can't have.

"Are you always this messy?" I ask.

"Hazard of the job. But it could be worse." There's a roughness to her voice as she lightly touches the scar on my cheek. Her hands are warm against my cold skin, and my gaze roams her gorgeous face as she inspects the welt, compliments of a high stick my rookie year.

I touch her chin, lift her head a little, until her lips part.

"Josie?"

"Yeah."

"I think Patrick is watching."

"Oh." She's about to turn her head toward the glass partitioner, but I stop her. "He's not usually here this—"

Before she can finish her sentence, I dip my head, and press my lips to hers. The second I taste her sweetness, the room closes in on me and my brain shuts down. Before I even realize what I'm doing, I slide my hand around her neck and take a fistful of her silky hair through the net. At first her lips are hesitant, then she slowly opens for me, and I swear up until this moment, I've never really kissed a woman before. Nope, what I was doing wasn't kissing. It wasn't even tasting, but now, now I'm devouring, and dammit, there is no way I'm going to get my fill.

The bell over the door jingles, and it snaps some sense back into me. I inch back and we stand there immobilized, breathless, and I can't speak for Josie, but I'm a quivering mess of need. Her fingers go to her lips, and her head turns slowly, taking in the showroom out front. She scans the crowd. "I...I don't see him." Her voice is as shaky as my body.

"Oh, sorry." I stand there and try to pull off casual, try to pretend that kiss didn't mess with every cell in my body, but I'm not sure I'm able to pull that off. "I thought I saw him."

"That's why you kissed me?"

"Yeah, sure, just to really drive the point home that we're a couple," I fib. I can't tell her the truth, that I've wanted to kiss her since I first set eyes on her. "We might have to do it again."

"Oh." Her eyes light up.

"For the charade." I gesture toward the glass. "I'm guessing a lot of people in the showroom saw us, and this is a small town. Small towns have rumor mills. We want this to get around."

"Yeah, yeah they do, and yes, yes we do." Her voice is rattled, flustered, full of need.

"You agree, then? We'll have to kiss a lot?"

Her chest rises and falls erratically. "I don't really see as we have a choice in the matter."

As I take in the sweet, gorgeous, innocent woman before me, one question jumps to the forefront of my brain.

What the hell are you doing, Brody?

6

JOSIE

He kissed me. NHL superstar Brody Tucker kissed me. And I liked it. Here it is hours later, and I can still feel the burning imprint on my lips. He said Patrick was watching, and he wanted to drive the point home that we were a couple, but was the kiss too much, going too far for this charade? Probably. Which means I should be more upset than I am. Truthfully, I could have stopped him. He didn't just pounce on me; the question of yes or no lingered in his eyes, and what did I do? I parted my lips in encouragement. I should regret it. Heck, I want to regret it. Kissing another man is wrong, right? It's a dishonor to my late husband.

I turn as Brody comes from my spare bedroom, Mabel right on his heels. "Look how good she's doing," he says as I take in his jeans, the nice way they hug his thighs, and the blue sweater that matches his eyes. "Such a fast learner, aren't you, girl?" He bends to pet her, rubbing those big hands of his all over her body as he gives her a kiss on her snout, and I have to say, I've had Mabel for six months now and never once was I jealous of her.

Get yourself together, girl.

"You're a dog whisperer, I get it." He laughs, and I say, "I'm sorry I'm a little late. I had this huge order come in. A great big shipment to numerous different addresses in Boston."

"Oh yeah?" He averts his gaze and for a second I think he's hiding something from me, but what on earth could he be hiding? We don't even really know one another and the fact that I invited a stranger to stay in my loft is absolutely crazy. *And why did you do that, Josie?* I guess it was something in his eyes, a strange mixture of honesty and vulnerability. I'm not one to trust so easily, but he's a friend of Declan's and Mabel is crazy about him.

"Since you're not going to tell me where we're going, am I dressed appropriately?"

His gaze leaves my face, trails over my sweater, and tight-fitting jeans. He scrubs his face and briefly closes his eyes like he's in total agony, and I bite back a smile. He said he didn't want to sleep with me, but he likes what he sees, and I shouldn't take such pleasure in it.

Truthfully, I haven't lived, haven't felt attractive in a long time. He reminds me I'm a woman with needs, but I can't give myself over to this man who is awakening things in me. He's a player who's leaving soon, and I've had enough heartache to last a lifetime.

"You're perfect," he says, and takes my coat from the closet to hand it to me.

I laugh, even though my insides are a little quivery from the comment. "I bet you say that to all the girls."

He looks me over again, his gaze slow and lingering. "Yeah, but this time I really mean it."

Another stupid little flutter goes through me. I poke him in the chest. "You really are a sweet talker, aren't you?"

He captures my finger and holds my hand to his chest. I revel in his strong heartbeat. "And you taste as sweet as you look."

My lips tingle at the reminder of our kiss, and he steps a bit closer, takes a strand of my hair and for the briefest of seconds, I think he's going to kiss me again. But what's surprising me most is how much I want him to. His head dips, and his throat makes a noise as he swallows. Our eyes meet, lock, and my lips automatically part. I wet them, and a growl crawls out of his throat at the exact same time Mabel barks. Brody backs up quickly, like the sound snapped some sense back into him, and I should be grateful for the interruption. *Should* being the key word here. Mabel, jealous of the attention Brody is giving me and not her, worms her way in between us, and Brody laughs and pats her head.

"You be a good girl, and I'll bring you back a treat." He straightens. "All set?"

I nod, pull on my winter coat, hat, scarf and mitts. I head to the door and look back to see if Brody is following, but he's standing there laughing and shaking his head. "Something funny?"

"You're not going to freeze to death, that's for sure."

"As long as there are no maniac drivers and potholes, I should be okay."

He groans at the reminder, and I laugh and swat him with the end of my scarf when he comes close. "You told me to dress warm, so I dressed warm."

He pulls on his coat, and hat, which has a pompom on it, and now it's my turn to laugh. "Your hat."

"You like it?" He shakes his head and the big gray pompom bounces. That, combined with the sexy smirk on his face, has to be the cutest thing I've ever seen.

"Anything for attention, huh?" I tease.

He gives a slow shake of his head, his lashes falling slowly, only to open again. "God, you get me."

"You're such a goof." I reach for his hat to tug on his pompom and his eyes go wide as he jerks away.

"You can't touch this," he says. "Not unless you're a Seattle Shooter."

"Is that right?" I ask, and purse my lips.

"Yup, Wes, the rookie on the team, is from Nova Scotia. It's damn cold there. Anyway, his mother made one for everyone on the team. These are our lucky hats. You're lucky you're even allowed to look at it."

"Athletes and their superstitions," I say with a laugh. "Well, it's a lovely hat, and I guess I'll have to stick with this one." I point to the light purple one I'm wearing. "Let's go."

We head downstairs and instead of going through the shop, we take the back door. The cool wind hits my face, the little part that is exposed, and I yelp.

"Come here," Brody says and pulls me into him. He walks me to his car, and opens the passenger door for me. I grin. Who knew he had old fashioned manners? He circles the front and there's another flutter in my stomach as he slides in next to me and smiles. "Ready?"

"Still not going to tell me where we're going?"

"Nope."

I just laugh as he starts the car and we head down the road. As he takes a few turns, my stomach tightens, because I'm beginning to guess where we're headed and exactly what he's up to. He pulls up to Santa Claus Land, and I take in a fast breath as memories bombard me.

"Hey, are you okay?" he asks reaching out to give my hand a little squeeze.

"Yeah, I just...used to come here." Every year my late husband and I would visit Santa Claus land. His favorite thing was the maze of Christmas trees. I haven't been able to visit the place since I moved here. I assumed it would be too hard, the memories too fresh. But sitting here now, listening to all the happy sounds, music, laughter, it surprisingly fills me with a sense of peace. "I'm okay," I assure Brody as he continues to scan my face, his brow furrowed with worry.

"You'd tell me if you weren't?"

"Yes."

"Good." He jumps from the car and I get out, snow crunching beneath my boots. He's smiling like a big kid, and I can't help but think he's up to something. He turns me and points to the horse-drawn sleigh ride, and I grin.

"Are we doing that?" Excitement moves through me. I've always wanted to take the sleigh ride, but Jon and I always seemed to miss it when we visited. Our timing was never right. Brody nods. "Are you going to be warm enough?"

He points to his head. "Uh, hat. Ain't no heat getting through that pompom. I'd wear this under my helmet if Coach let me."

I laugh and whack his stomach. I do love his sense of humor and no one has made me laugh, made me feel young and happy and feminine in a very long time. We head toward the horse, and Brody speaks with the driver for a second. He helps me into the seat, and I look behind us. "Where is everyone?"

"Just us."

I eye him, and angle my head. "You planned this for just us?"

"Still hate surprises?" he asks, and my gaze drops to his mouth, wanting to kiss him again.

"As a general rule, yes, but you did good."

"I'm such a great boyfriend. Do you have any idea how lucky you are?"

I laugh again. "Maybe you're the lucky one."

"You're right. You're a catch. My catch." I eye him and he shrugs. "For the next few days anyway," he clarifies and reminds me that this fake relationship comes with an expiry date, which I hadn't forgotten.

I settle next to him, my insides a squishy mess as he grabs the blanket to cover us. I breathe in the night air and stare at the star-studded sky as the horse takes us down the snowy road.

I turn to Brody. "I've always wanted to do this."

"Why haven't you?"

I shrug. "I don't know. I guess I just never got around to it, and it's more for families and couples. I mean, I have friends here...I just probably wouldn't ask them to do this."

"What else do you want to do that you haven't done yet?"

Honestly, there are so many things for couples to do in this town, I have no idea where to begin.

"Wait," he says. "Don't tell me. I'd rather figure it out on my own."

I grin up at him as the horse trots along, and we both go quiet, enjoying nature and the night sky. Soon enough, the horse slows and I sit up a little straighter and glance around. I spot Liam in the tree lot.

"So this was all about getting you a tree."

He grins at me. "Maybe it's about getting *you* a tree."

"Hey, I thought the tree was about you." I poke him and he snatches up my hand.

"It is, and you and Miss Mabel. I was thinking we could get a Douglas fir."

I stare at him for a moment, incredulously. Has he been asking around about me? "How did you know Douglas fir was my favorite?"

"I didn't. It's my favorite."

Not sure if I believe him or not—but why on earth would he lie about that?—I stand. "Come on. Let's go find a tree."

"Can we get one with the down swept branches?"

"Is there any other kind?" I ask. Okay, he for sure has been asking around. There is no way we have the exact same taste in Christmas trees.

He jumps up, and how can I not smile at his enthusiasm? It's contagious and warming, and fills me with life and laughter. With a kind of grace I could only hope for, he hops from the carriage and I'm about to do the same when he puts his hands on my waist and helps me down. I land on my feet, my body flush with his and I stand there breathless for a moment. His head dips and my throat goes dry. Seconds pass, but it feels more like minutes.

I turn and catch a few people watching us. "Ah, we should... ah...tree."

"Right," he says and quickly steps back, moments before I ignite and burn the entire lot down. We walk to the display, and Liam comes and greets us.

"Hey Josie," he says, and his jaw drops when he turns to Brody. "Brody Tucker," he says. "I heard you were in town."

"Hey man, how are you doing?" Liam stands there, completely star-struck, so Brody carries the conversation. "We're here for a tree, obviously," Brody says. "Nice lot you have here."

Liam shakes his head, and I can't help but chuckle. "Yeah, right sure. Just holler if you need any help. Wait, do you think I could get an autograph sometime?"

"How about right now?"

Liam produces a pen and a piece of paper and Brody scribbles his name. Liam is like a giggling child when he hands it back.

"We'll find our own way," Brody says. Liam is still standing there, a goofy grin on his face, as Brody takes my hand and gives a tug.

"Is it always like that for you?" I ask.

He shrugs. "I don't mind. I'm nothing without my fans."

I nod, liking that about him. We move through the lot, and every now and then, Brody stops to have his picture taken with some people. I stand back and watch him. He's especially good to the kids, dropping to the ground despite the cold snow, and chatting with them eye to eye.

He finishes up and shoves his hands into his coat as he walks back to me, a smile on his face, and a gleam in his gorgeous eyes.

"You're good with the kids." He shrugs like it's nothing, but I'm not buying it. I nudge him, and he turns the conversation to me. "Do you like kids?"

I nod. "Sure."

"You want kids of your own?"

My throat tightens, pain making it hard to talk. "I used to envision a future with kids."

"You don't now?"

I give a fast shake of my head and redirect. "You'll be a good dad." He makes a face like I said something so ludicrous, he doesn't know how to process. "What?"

"I know nothing about being a dad."

"Kayley told me your dad is an NHL hall of famer."

"She'd be right." He walks toward a tree and touches the needles. Even with his back to me, I can sense the hurt in him. I guess he and his dad aren't close and that explains why he's at his friend's house for Christmas instead of being with his own family, and I'll never forget the hurt he was trying to hide when he talked about all the 'Moms' in his life. My heart tightens and the sudden urge to give him an amazing holiday comes over me. I didn't really celebrate last year, after losing my husband. Celebrating felt wrong, living and enjoying life felt wrong, but maybe I can do this for Brody. He glances back at me. "What do you think of this one?"

"Come on." I grab his hand and tug, and take him to the back of the tree farm where they keep the biggest and fullest trees. His eyes go wide.

"We'll never fit any of these into your place."

"Oh, ye of little faith." I point to the biggest Douglas fir. "I like this one right here." I lean into him, and he glances down at me. "I think it's perfect."

"Perfect, yeah," he says, his eyes on me giving me the sense he's talking about me, not the tree. A fine shiver goes through me and he tugs me to him to keep me warm, but the shiver had nothing to do with the cold and everything to do with the man gazing at me, making me remember what it was like to really live, to be happy. Joy wells up inside of me, taking me by surprise, and tears threaten to fall, my emotions all over the place today—because of Brody.

But I can't fall for him. Not only is he only here for the holiday, he's a man with a reputation, and I'm a woman with a late husband. I barely know Brody. Sure, he's staying with me, and sure he makes me laugh and feel alive again. I don't believe in love at first sight, and our first meeting was nothing to write home about. It could be a funny story down the road for the grandchildren. Brody was right about that. That thought brings on a small smile, but I quickly wipe it away. This is wrong. Just so wrong.

Then why does it feel so right?

BRODY

F our days until Christmas Eve:

Morning light shines into the bedroom, and I pull myself awake. After last night's horse-drawn carriage ride and picking out a tree, we had fun at Santa Claus Land, and came back here to watch a Hallmark movie. I might have made a big deal about Josie *forcing* me to watch, but whatever. We all know I like sappy Christmas movies, and watching it with Josie made it even better. In fact, doing anything with Josie by my side breathes new life into me, into everything we're doing. I smile as I think of her. I love the way her laugh wraps around me, and how the warm chocolatey scent of her skin drives me crazy for a taste. I swear if I don't soon get another, I might spontaneously combust.

Picking a tree out with her last night filled me with a warmth I'm not familiar with, and I love that she decided on a ginormous Douglas fir that will eat up her entire living room. My

Christmases were mostly spent alone, and the one thing I learned early on is that it's not the tree, or the gifts under it— it's the people around it that make Christmas special. I can't wait to sit around the big Douglas fir tree with Josie and Mabel on Christmas morning. The tree should be delivered later today, and since Josie doesn't have a single ornament, or if she does, they're in storage somewhere, I'm going to get supplies to make our own tonight before the tree gets delivered.

Yesterday she had to work late because of me. I was the one to put all the orders in, delivered to friends and family in the Boston area. She had to get a new phone because of my stupidity, and since I can't come right out and tell her I found hers, or give her the money to pay for the replacement, buying a shit-ton of chocolate was my only option to make up for my momentary lack of judgement. A measure of guilt eats at me as I look at my travel bag on the floor, her phone tucked safely inside it.

As if sensing I'm awake, Miss Mabel claws at the door, and I jump up, tug on some clothes and greet her quietly. I'm sure Josie hasn't slept in since getting the dog, and I like helping her out. Being with Mabel isn't a hardship. She's a loveable girl who just needs a bit of training.

Her tail wags wildly when I open the door, and I hush her. "Let's let your mom sleep in," I say. The word mom makes me smile. Yesterday Josie said I'd be a good dad and I balked at the idea. The truth is, I want what my friends have. I just don't know how to get it, and there's something about me that drives women away. Everyone eventually leaves. Look at my own mother, and my stepmothers. I was never enough for them.

Would I be enough for Josie?

Whoa! Where the hell did that thought come from? I barely know her. Sure, I like everything that I do know about her, and it's easy to tell she's a good person with a good heart. Which makes me wonder why she's still single. She's a real catch and any guy would be lucky to call her his.

I'd be lucky to call her mine...and not in a pretend way.

My stomach tightens. Jesus, am I really thinking about this?

I shake my head to clear it. I'm going down a rabbit hole I have no right to go down. She's a nice girl—not at all the grouch I thought she was when Declan picked her out for me. I don't want to get involved with her. Don't want to? Correction, I *do* want to, I just can't. I mess everything up and I don't want to mess her life up.

What if I didn't screw things up with her? What if I did everything right and she left anyway?

"Come on, girl," I whisper, and grab Mabel's leash. I text Josie to let her know we're heading out, so she doesn't wake up and worry I've dognapped Mabel. I quietly open the door and we head outside into the cold, which Mabel seems to love. She jumps into the snow, runs her face through it, and I take joy in the sight of her playing. We walk to the park, and do some training, then off to the grocery store for tree supplies. The streets are quiet this Sunday morning and I'm able to move through them quickly without stopping for too many autographs.

By the time we make it back to the loft, Josie is pouring a generous amount of coffee into a big mug. I take one look at her in the kitchen, her hair a tumbled mess down her back, and wearing baggy PJ pants and a T-shirt. She turns to me as I admire her, a smile on her face. My heart lurches. When was the last time someone looked at me like they were truly happy to see me? I've been with lots of different women, but the warm, happy smile on Josie's face is genuine, unrehearsed, and it hits me differently. She hands me her cup of coffee and a strange, unfamiliar feeling courses through my veins. It wraps around my heart and tugs me off balance.

My God, I really like this girl. Is it possible that we could be more than friends, that I wouldn't mess it up, that she wouldn't eventually leave?

"Thank you," she says, her voice soft and sleepy, and so damn sexy I bite the inside of my cheek to keep myself in check. I hold the cup up, and while I'm working to keep my shit together, I can't help but imagine what it would be like waking up with her every day, coming home to her every night.

"I'm the one who should be thanking you. I haven't had a cup yet. Didn't want to wake you up by banging around in the kitchen."

"You're sweet." I stand there dumbfounded. I've been called a lot of things, but never sweet. Sweet talker yes, but not sweet. She bends to pet Miss Mabel. "Hey girl, did you have fun with Brody?" Mabel's tail wags harder and she abandons her mom, and comes back to me. "Traitor."

"She knows a good thing when she sees it," I tease.

"Yeah, she does."

My head snaps up, and I catch the soft smile, the almost dreamy look on her face when our eyes meet. She takes a breath and exhales slowly, her focus shifting to the bag in my hand—like she needs the distraction. "What did you buy?"

I hold the bag up. "Tree decorations. I wasn't sure if you had any, and I thought we could do homemade stuff."

I set the bag on the counter, and take out the popcorn, and cranberries. She goes perfectly still when she sees them. Shit, she hates this idea. "We can get bulbs, I just thought..." I'm about to pack the stuff back up again when she puts her hand on my arm.

"No, I love it, Brody." She lifts her head, her brow furrowed. "It's funny, you seem to know everything I like."

I shrug. "Maybe we just like the same things."

She picks up the bag of cranberries. "This is exactly how I like to decorate." She smiles, and I guess she's remembering happy times.

"When I was little, we used to make gingerbread men and hang them too."

"We can do that, but I suggest we hang them high." I point to Mabel. "Otherwise, we're likely to wake up to a very full dog, and a bare tree."

She laughs at that and the sound goes through me. "I never thought of that." Her nose crinkles "Maybe this year we'll pass on that idea. Perhaps we can do it next year, when she gets older, and is better trained."

Next year? Will I be back in town next year? Is she suggesting that or is it simply wishful thinking on my part?

"I don't know, Josie." I make a tsking sound. "I think ginger-bread is tempting no matter a dog's age, or a guy's age. I'm twenty-eight, and I can't be trusted around them."

"You are kind of like a big kid." She chuckles quietly. "I like that, though."

My phone pings, and I pull it from my back pocket. I read the message from Declan. I lift my head to find Josie still staring at me. "Do you have skates?" I ask.

"I do. Why?"

"Because I thought we'd go downhill skiing." She frowns. "I'm joking." I hold my hand up before she can say anything. "Smart ass, I know. Let me try again. Want to go skating? Declan and Nikki are heading to the outside rink, wherever that is, after lunch." She hesitates, and when my heart sinks, it becomes abundantly clear that I hate the idea of not spending every waking moment with her—as well as sleeping, but that's a different story. "You must have to work?"

"I can take today off. The store is open because it's the holidays, but I have part time staff."

"You just don't like skating?"

"I just haven't done it in a while."

"We don't have to. I'll tell Declan we're busy."

"No," she says quickly. "First, I'm not keeping you from your friend, and second, I think it sounds like a fun idea, and it's been a long time since I've done fun things."

"Sweet," I say, and she stands there and grins at me as I text Declan back. "Why are you looking at me like that?"

"You're just so full of energy, and you take pleasure in everything. It's like the world is just a big playground to you."

I tuck my phone away. "You say that like it's a bad thing."

"Not at all, Brody. I like it a lot, and to be honest..." She looks down for a second, a wave of sadness overcoming her. "It's just...everything about you is a reminder that life is meant to be lived."

Now it's my turn to frown, not really understanding what life events took her to a place where she felt she wasn't living. I hate that. I hate that she feels life is passing her by. I'm about to pull her into my arms and offer comfort, when she turns from me.

"I'll make us some breakfast." I shut my mouth as she purposely switches subjects. She doesn't want to talk about her life, and that's fine. I won't push, but I damn well plan to make every moment with her count, and bring a smile to her face every day while I'm here. If past events have been holding her back, I plan to help her move forward.

"How about we go out? We can grab some bagel sandwiches at Coffee Klatch."

"That sounds nice, actually." She runs her fingers through her hair. "Wait, how do you know bagel sandwiches are my favorite?"

"I have my ways," I tease. I honestly had no idea. I suggested them because they're my favorite.

She angles her head and eyes me. "Who have you been talking to?"

I laugh. "No one. Honest."

"Hmmm..." She laughs, but there is doubt in her eyes. "I'll let it go for now." She glances at her pajamas. "Just let me get cleaned up. I'll be super-fast."

I stare after her as she heads down the hall, and after a fast shower, and a quick blow-dry she reappears dressed in jeans and a loose-fitting sweater. Her face, free of makeup, looks freshly scrubbed and her hair is loose and still a bit damp around her shoulders, giving her a sexy, just crawled out of bed look. I like it. A lot. I just wish I was the one crawling out of bed with her.

"That was fast," I say.

"I'm very low maintenance."

She winks at me and goes about filling Mabel's bowls with water and food. I laugh at that. Most girls I hang out with wouldn't be caught dead without makeup. Which is ridiculous. It's not the makeup that makes a person attractive, just like it shouldn't be the jersey I wear that appeals to women. Josie doesn't seem like the type to want a guy because he wears an NHL jersey.

"Do you watch hockey?" I ask, the question jumping out of my mouth.

"I used to. I don't anymore. I enjoyed watching Declan because he's from Holiday Peak."

She puts her jacket on and tugs on a hat. "Josie, can I ask you something?"

She looks a bit hesitant as we say goodbye to Mabel and head out the door. "I guess."

"Seems to me you used to do a lot of things. What changed?"

She goes quiet, too quiet as we step out into the cold and walk toward Coffee Klatch, and once again, I realize I hit a nerve. "I'm sorry. You don't have to answer that."

"I lost my husband," she says so quietly, I'm not even sure I heard her right. "Last year."

The pain in her eyes hurts my heart. "I'm...so sorry, Josie. I didn't know."

"Of course, you didn't. How could you?" She looks around the snow-covered streets, the lost look on her face hurting my heart. "I moved here for a fresh start."

"But have you...started?"

She looks at the ground. "No, not really."

All the pieces known as Josie—her not moving forward, not having fun, no kids in the future—begin to fall into place, and something powerful, something almost blinding surges inside me. The need to protect her, do for her...be there for her, nearly takes me to my knees.

"Josie?"

"Yeah."

Loss is hard and she might not be ready to move forward just yet, so I'm careful with my next question. "Do you want to start again?"

Her smile is wobbly as she glances up at me. "I'm not sure what I want, Brody. All I know is I've been having fun with you, doing things I stopped doing, because maybe I shouldn't be having fun, shouldn't be with another guy. Does that even make any sense?"

I nod in quiet understanding. My mother left me, she didn't die, but I understand loss. "You don't want to dishonor his memory."

She nods, and blinks rapidly, no doubt working to keep the tears away.

"I didn't know your late husband, but I can only imagine he was a great man. He'd have to be for you to choose him, and because he was great, don't you think he'd want you to move forward, find a happy life for yourself?"

She glances at her boots. "I...just don't know."

"Did he ever say that to you? Is it not something you guys discussed?"

"No."

"Was his death sudden?"

"Car accident. He died at the hospital. He..." She stops talking like she can't bring herself to say what's eating her up inside.

We stop outside Coffee Klatch. "I know in my heart he'd want you to be happy and not let life pass you by. You want that too, don't you?"

"I want—" Before she can finish, the door opens and out walks Patrick.

"Good morning," he says with a smile. I tug Josie closer, and much different from our first embrace, her body softens, melts against mine—something inside her shifting. While I'm not sure what she was going to say to me a second ago, there's a part of me that understands she wants to live life, but is too afraid. I'm a chicken shit myself when it comes to relationships. But maybe I don't want to be anymore. Maybe I'm just damn tired of that bullshit, and maybe, just maybe, the reason behind all that is the woman in my arms.

So, what are you going to do about that, Brody?

8

JOSIE

I wobble in my skates and I'm seconds from going down when Brody puts his strong arm around me and anchors me to his body. I laugh up at him, loving the power and strength in his touch, the way he's quick to come to my rescue. It's been a long time since a man's touch gave me a sense of comfort and security.

"It's not like riding a bike," I joke.

"You like biking?"

I nod. "I used to."

"We can do that later."

I shake my head. "You're crazy. The streets are snow-covered. If I don't break my neck on this rink, I'll definitely break it on a bike."

"Where's your sense of adventure?"

"You have enough for the two of us," I say, as some young kid speed skates past us, leaving us in his dust. "I hate that kid," I say and laugh.

Brody laughs with me. "Future NHL star in the making right there, my friend." I smile, happy that Brody and I are friends.

I want more...

Oh boy.

"Brody," Declan calls from the other side of the rink, a group of kids around him. "How about a pick-up game?" He glances at me, his eyes questioning.

"While I appreciate you not wanting to leave me alone to face plant, go play. I'm going to get a hot chocolate and introduce my backside to that bench right there."

He laughs, and it's so contagious that I laugh with him. Before I even realize what's happening, he bends and puts his lips on mine. His mouth is cold at first, but it doesn't take long for it to warm up as he deepens the kiss. I stand there, immobilized, unable to think or breathe, aware of our public display of affection, and the attention it's garnering. He finally breaks the kiss and backs up.

"What was that for?" I ask, my voice a low, breathless whisper. At least with all my layers on, he can't see the chain reactions going on in my body.

He looks past my shoulders, a grin toying with the corners of his mouth. "I thought I saw Patrick."

I glance over my shoulder. "I don't see him."

"That man is like Houdini, one minute he's there, the next he's gone."

"Uh, huh," I say, and he gives me a sexy grin as he skates away, backward, putting my wobbly efforts to shame. My lips continue to tingle as I glide to the boards. I search the crowd again, even though I know Patrick is nowhere to be found. Brody kissed me because he wanted to. My insides flutter, and while the kiss was a surprise, I can't deny it was a welcome one. I make my way to the pop-up hot chocolate stand and get a drink, with extra marshmallows, of course.

I plop down onto one of the benches and sip as I scan the rink, catching sight of Declan and Brody set up on one end, playing hockey with a group of kids of all ages. Brody takes a shot, even though he plays defense in the NHL, and the puck goes into the net. He throws his hands up.

"I have no equal," he says, and Declan grabs him and puts him into a headlock, encouraging the kids to rub their knuckles over his head. Laughter fills the air and my insides squeeze, loving his antics, and how much the kids love him for them. My ovaries clench, the old biological clock ticking, when he picks up one of the smaller kids and starts skating toward the net, like he's going to use him for a puck. The other kids chase him down, and I can't help but laugh.

"Mind if I sit here?"

I glance up to find Nikki standing there, a hot chocolate in her hand. I don't know her well, other than she's a hair stylist at Chatters, where gossip truly runs rampant. She's come into the store a few times, and she's always pleasant and sweet. I tap the bench.

"I'd love the company."

She sits next to me, and we both go quiet as we watch the excitement on the ice. "So, you and Brody, huh?" she says breaking the silence.

"It's not what you think," I say, my voice low, not wanting anyone around us to overhear. "He's just helping me out with something."

She chuckles. "I heard he's working with Mabel." There's a gleam in her eye that says she knows more is going on, but I appreciate her not pushing it. People are going to think what they want, and we fed the rumor mill with that kiss. "It's nice to see you with someone, Josie." Her voice is full of kindness and sincerity. "From what Declan says, Brody is one of the good guys."

I nod in agreement and warmth spreads through my chest. He *is* one of the good guys. Even Miss Mabel thinks so. "He's got quite the reputation, though. You know, as a sweet talker."

She laughs, and her big blue eyes glisten. "I think it's just going to take the right woman for him to settle down."

"What about Declan?" I ask. Brody mentioned something about Declan spending time with his girl, Nikki. "Are you two a couple?"

She gives a humorless chuckle. "He's known as the heartbreaker, Josie." She takes a sip of her drink and stares straight ahead. "We're just friends. We go way back."

I get the sense she might want more, but go quiet. If she doesn't want to talk about it, I'm not going to say anything.

Brody comes skating over, tugging an empty water bottle from his jacket. He cracks the lid, tips it, but nothing comes out.

I hand him my cup. "It's hot, but it's wet."

He takes a sip, hands it back, and wipes his mouth with the back of his glove. "Hey Nikki," he says. "Nice to finally meet you."

"You too," she says, and Brody looks back at me. He drops to his knees and bites the tip of his gloves to remove them.

"You can't go back out there with this untied." He puts my foot on his lap and takes my laces into his big hands. Even though it's an innocent gesture, everything in what he's doing sends warmth surging through me, and it's weird, because even though there's nothing intimate in tying my laces, it feels far more intimate than that last kiss, creating a new kind of comfort and closeness between us. Nikki chuckles. I turn to her as she sits there staring at me, a wildly wicked grin on her face.

"I actually wasn't planning on going back out there," I manage to say to Brody. "I'm happy to sit here and watch you guys play."

"You sure?" Blue eyes meet mine, and my traitorous body ignites. He leans into me, his lips close, the scent of hot chocolate on his breath. "You want to sit it out?"

"I'm perfectly happy right here."

He moves closer, and my heart beats a little faster as his lips close over mine. He gives me a fast kiss, like it's the most natural thing in the world, like it's something we do all the time, and when he breaks it, I can't quite seem to fill my lungs.

"Just let me go score one more goal and I'll be back." He touches my face, gently runs his thumb over my cheek, and my body ignites.

I try to sound normal, unaffected, but fail miserably. "They're kids, Brody. For God's sake, let one of them score."

He rubs his knuckles over his head. "Every single one of those knuckleheads gave me a knuckle sandwich." His indignant attitude—fake as it is—combined with his childlike enthusiasm, pulls a laugh from Nikki and me. "Now they're going to get what they have coming to them."

"My God, he's funny," Nikki says when he skates away, and I can't seem to tear my gaze away. I sit there grinning, like the village idiot no doubt, my insides a hot mess from that kiss and his adorable playfulness.

Nikki gives me a little nudge. "You know, you two make a cute couple."

"We're not..." I let my words fall off. We're not a real couple, we're just pretending to be one. Sure, our chemistry is off the charts, and now suddenly he's kissing me every chance he gets. We might be faking it, yet I can't help but think there is more going on here. As I consider that, something inside me shifts, softens, allows me to entertain the idea of us being a real couple. An incredible warmth goes through me, melting my darkest corners. Was he right when he said my late husband would have wanted me to move on, to be happy? I never wanted to, never had the urge to until Brody. I've kept myself so closed off, life just passing me by, but Brody has given me a taste of what it's like to live again...feel again.

Out on the ice, Brody scores and his cheers are louder than anyone's, and the kids are loving it. So are the adults. I don't miss the way the single ladies, not to mention a few of the married ones, are admiring him. A sudden burst of jealousy moves through me, but I have no right to feel it. He isn't mine and I'm not his.

"Yeah, you're not a couple at all," Nikki says, and I turn to her to find her grinning, like she knows something I don't.

"We're friends," I clarify. "Like you and Declan."

She exhales and nods, "Yeah, like me and Declan." She looks down and there's a deep sadness about her when she adds, "But unlike me and Declan, he just kissed you. Or did I just imagine that?"

My hand flies to my lips. "We're just pretending." I can tell myself that all I like, but there was nothing fake about Brody's kiss. It was sweet and passionate and natural and easy. It felt...right. I wait for the guilt to hit, and it does, just not as hard as the first couple of times.

"The last time I saw a pretend kiss like that was at a wedding, right after the couple said, 'I do.'"

"I...wait...what?"

She leans into me. "None of this is my business, but you should try to be honest with yourself. We don't always get second chances at love, and I'd hate to see you let something slip out of your hands." With that, she pushes to her feet and makes her way to the rink. She skates over to the guys, and Brody turns to me. His smile turns me inside out, and I know I'm in real trouble here.

He comes over to me. "Want to head back, see if the tree's been delivered?"

"Sounds like a plan," I say, and wave to my friend Mabel as she glides onto the ice. A sense of place and family comes over me. All these people took me in when I was lost, and they've made this town a home for me. Now it's time for me to make my loft a home too, and as I take in Brody's smile, I realize there isn't anyone I'd rather decorate my tree with today.

Does that mean I'm ready for a second chance at love?

My heart thumps a little harder and the air whips at my face as we make the short trek back to my place on foot, and when we reach the back door, and find our gorgeous tree is leaning against the house, I squeal a little. "It's here!"

"Get the door for me, and I'll carry it up."

I open the door and let him go first. At the landing, I slip around him, our bodies touching, sending heat arching through me, and I open the loft door. Mabel is right there, greeting us with a wagging tail.

"Back up, girl." She backs up, giving Brody room to carry the tree to the living room. I set the stand for him and he puts the tree in. I drop and tighten the screws to hold it upright. We both stand back and admire the oversized tree that eats up my whole living room.

"I love it." Mabel barks at the tree, not knowing what to make of it.

"Hey girl," Brody says and drops to his knees to pet her. "It's just a tree, nothing to be afraid of." Mabel settles a little and leans into Brody, her big protector. "Why don't I take her out for a minute before we get started?"

"I'm sure she'd appreciate that." He stands and I say, "I would too."

"Gotta keep my girls happy." He makes a huffing sound. "Being the world's most awesome boyfriend sure takes a lot of work."

"I'll have a nice hot cup of coffee waiting for you when you get back." Without even realizing what I'm doing, I lift my mouth to his and go up on my toes. He puts his hands on my arms, and presses his lips to mine. I part for him, and a moan crawls out of my throat as he slides his tongue in to play with mine. A loud bark interrupts the intimate moment, and I go back down on my feet.

"What was that for?" he asks, the blue in his eyes a bit darker, the want and need reflecting mine.

Without even turning, I jerk my thumb toward my window. "I was sure Patrick was peeking."

His grin is slow, devilish. "He's been doing that a lot."

"I know. I don't know what his problem is."

"Me neither." He exhales loudly, feigning frustration, like this whole thing is a hardship. "But if we have to keep on kissing to keep this ruse going, then we have to do what we have to do."

"It makes me want to dig my heels in, you know." My lips twitch as I try not to smile. "Really drive the fact home that we're in a relationship."

He nods in agreement. "I'm stubborn like that too. The more he pushes, the more I want to push back. If push comes to shove, and we're left with no choice, I'll take you to that bedroom. I'll do what it takes to drive the point home." Mabel barks. "But first, a potty trip."

With my insides soaring, I laugh and give him a shove. "Go."

As soon as they leave, I put on a fresh pot of coffee and put a bag of popcorn into the microwave. I catch my reflection in the window and notice the smile on my face. It's been a long time since I've smiled so hard, or felt any kind of lightness inside of me. I glance outside and laugh as Brody throws snowballs and Mabel tries to catch them. My heart pinches. She's going to miss him when he leaves.

I'm going to miss him when he leaves.

The microwave beeps and pulls me back, and by the time Brody comes inside with Mabel, I have the string, popcorn and cranberries all ready to go. I put coffee and cookies on a tray and carry them into the living room. Brody and Mabel follow. As I admire my beautiful tree, Brody places his hand on the small of my back. Warmth spreads through me, the heat from his touch, and the magic of the holiday season like a soothing balm to my heart. I take a breath, and for the first time in a long time, it doesn't hurt to expand my lungs.

Mabel sniffs the tree, and when a branch springs back and bops her on the nose, she barks. "Come on, girl," Brody says and guides her to her big comfy pillow. She snarls at the tree, then stretches and settles on her bed for a sleep. As Brody drops to the sofa, I can't help but think an afternoon nap would be nice, too. I can't remember the last time I treated myself to a quick one. A nap, I mean, not a quickie. Not sex. I'm not thinking about sex.

Liar.

My God, ever since he said he'd take me to the bedroom—correction, ever since he gave me a cold, slushy shower—I haven't been able to stop thinking about sex. *Why is that, Josie?* Oh, probably because the hottest guy on the planet wants me as much as I want him, and he couldn't look anymore adorable as he begins to string together popcorn, shoving a handful into his mouth.

He smiles up at me. "Everything okay?"

"Just tired."

"You can nap if you want. We can do this later."

"I actually think that's a great idea." My heart pounds against my chest because I can't believe what I'm about to do...say. "Are you tired?"

"Nah, I'm okay."

"Oh," I say and his head lifts. I instantly know the second understanding hits by the way his eyes widen. He jumps up and the bowl of popcorn spills to the floor. His gaze goes from me to the popcorn, back to me, and there's almost a panic about him, like he might have just ruined the moment.

"Shit...I..."

"Mabel likes popcorn," I tell him and hold my hand out. "So, you are tired, then. Is that what you're trying to tell me?"

"Yeah, exhausted," he explains, knowing exactly what I'm asking. "Spent. Can't even keep my eyes open."

I laugh at his enthusiasm and want careens through my blood, hitting every erogenous zone on the way. "Oh, that's too bad, because I was thinking—"

"Forget about that," he says so quickly, I stiffen. Is he having second thoughts? There's an intensity about him that I've never seen before. Oh, God have I been reading this all wrong? Was he only kissing me because he thought Patrick could see? Did I make a fool of myself in the kitchen when it was clear Patrick was nowhere in the vicinity? I'm about to back up when he captures my arm to hold me in place. "Don't tell me what you were thinking." He picks me up and I gasp as he stalks down the hall. He practically kicks my bedroom door open, slams it shut and presses me against it. "Show me instead."

9

BRODY

y heart beats wildly in my chest as she runs her hands down my back, her lush breasts pressed against my chest, her nipples hard enough to score our clothes. Fuck, I have never wanted—needed—to be with anyone as much as I need to be with her. It's frightening and exciting all at the same time.

With one arm around her, anchoring her tight against me so she doesn't slip from my hips, I brush her hair back, my gaze moving over her face to take in the lust dancing in her eyes. While I want her—fuck, it might take more than the Shooters' defensive end to pull her away from me—I need to know for sure this is what she wants.

"Josie," I whisper, as her feet slide from around my back until she's standing before me, gazing up at me with half-lidded eyes so full of desire I could fucking weep. I say her name again, and the lust retreats for a second, allowing understanding to take center stage.

"I want you, Brody." She bumps against my thick cock, and I moan. "I want *this*," she reassures me, after reading the concern in my eyes. "The fact that you're worried about me, makes me want this—you—all the more."

"What can I say, I'm a good boyfriend." I'm making light of things, but there isn't anything light about this moment. If I work really hard, I might be able to convince myself this is nothing more than sex between two people who barely know each other—been there, done that—but this warmth in my chest makes me think it's a pivotal moment, like we're crossing some imaginary line, and that is fucking scary because I don't want to hurt her when I mess this all up. Not that we're trying for a relationship here. I know better.

"Brody," she murmurs. "Just us, just tonight, or just this week. Let's not overthink this. Instead, let's just have some fun. Like I said, it's been far too long since I just let go."

"Letting go is good."

She grins, liking my answer, and slides into playful mode. "Okay, good boyfriend, what is it you wanted me to show you?"

I press my thumb to her bottom lip and she surprises me by sticking her tongue out to lick it.

"Jesus," I growl, and shove my thumb into her hot mouth. She sucks me, and I nearly blow a load in my pants. I swallow and work to keep my shit together, but she has a small grin on her face. She likes what she's doing to me. "Show me what you were thinking." My thumb falls from her mouth, and I instantly miss her heat as she steps back, moving toward her bed. "Show me what you like," I demand in a soft voice.

Her knees hit the bed, and as if the contact jolts something loose inside, her body stiffens, and she takes a fast breath. "Hey." Her brow crinkles and she looks down. In two long strides, I'm right there, standing before her, my wet thumb under her chin, lifting her gaze to mine. "What is it?"

"It's...nothing." She smiles, but I'm not having any of that.

"Talk to me, Josie." I take her hands in mine. I hold her tight, gently rub my thumbs over her wrists. "We don't go any further until you tell me what just happened there." She frowns. "We're about to get naked and I'm about to put my cock inside you. It doesn't get any more real than that, so please, be honest with me."

"It's...it's been a long time."

Warmth for the woman who's standing before me, exposing her vulnerability, trusting me with it, fills my heart, and makes me fall just a little bit for her. "I know, it's okay." I cup her cheek and she leans into my hand.

"My late husband...he was the only man I'd ever been with. What if I'm...What if I don't remember what I like?" Her loud gulp fills the quiet of the room. "And you...you've been with a lot of women, what if I dis—"

"Are you fucking kidding me right now?"

Her eyes widen. "What?"

I grab her hips, and tug her to me, pressing my hard as granite cock into her stomach. "I want you. If you tell me no, fine. I'll respect that. But just know that I'll be leaving this room and won't be back for a long time."

"A...long time?"

"Yeah, I'll be in the shower tugging one or twenty out." I soften my voice when her eyes light with pleasure. "I want you. I have since I first set eyes on you. There is nothing you could do to disappoint me, and come to think of it, it's not so bad that you might have forgotten what you like." She angles her head, curiosity in her eyes. I pull on the hem of her sweater and slide my hands underneath to brush the warm, soft skin of her stomach. She sucks in a fast breath, a pink flush on her cheeks. "I think it's going to be a lot of fun exploring your gorgeous body and discovering all your wants and needs." I lightly brush my lips over hers. "You said a few times now that it's been a long time since you had fun, right?"

"That's right."

"You think this will be fun?"

"I think if you don't get me naked soon, I might spontaneously combust."

I chuckle at that, knowing the feeling all too well. "Lift your arms."

She does as I ask and I peel her sweater over her head. Static makes her hair stand on end and she couldn't look any more adorable than she does right now. But that thought leaves my head the second my gaze drops to take in her lush breasts, mainly the way her pink nipples are poking against her lacy bra. I wet my lips, and she moans in response, arching into me as I cup the sides of her breasts and lightly run my fingers over the soft material, wanting to go at her caveman-style, but I force myself to slow down and savor every goddamn moment, because everything in my brain is telling me Josie is worth cherishing, and might fuck me over in dangerous ways.

She slides her hands behind her back and unhooks her bra. It falls forward and her gorgeous tits spill into my hands. I massage them, and her head falls back, her hair tumbling down her back. Jesus, she's so gorgeous.

"That is so good," she says, the deep longing and need in her voice tugging at me. I bend forward to take one beautifully hard nipple into my mouth and breathe in the sweet scent of her skin. It's an aphrodisiac. Powerful. Addicting. Mind-fuck-ing-blowing. I lick her nipple and suck the tight bud into my mouth, and her nails scrape against my scalp, like she's clam-oring for me. No worries, sweetness. I plan to give you more —everything. Well, not everything. I can't give my heart.

I move my mouth to her other breast. "Do you like this, Josie?" I ask, and glance up at her. She looks back at me, and I grin, taking in her dreamlike state as she slowly nods. I put my hand between her legs, lightly brush her sex through her pants and she gasps. "I can't wait to discover what you like down here."

"Yes, please..."

I lick her other nipple, then press open-mouthed kisses to her stomach as I sink to my knees, and put my mouth against her jeans. I exhale, warming her hot pussy through her clothes and she whimpers and wobbles, a little unstable on her feet.

I pop the button, slowly slide her zipper down, and her sexy little mewling sounds let me know how desperate she is for my touch. I tug her pants down, just enough to expose her damp curls. Her warm, aroused scent fills my nostrils and I breathe her into my lungs. With her legs tight together, I slide my tongue between her snug lips, tasting her sweetness as I go from bottom to top, until I reach her swollen clit. I lightly tease it with my tongue, and it quivers in response.

"Brody," she gasps. "Brody, that is...God, that is good."

"Let's see what else you like." I nudge her until she's sitting on the bed, her gorgeous breasts free, her pants snug around her thighs. My racing heart skips a few beats as I take pleasure in the seductive sight before me. How did I get so fucking lucky?

"I want to see what you like," she says, and reaches for me. She puts her hand over my bulge and rubs gently.

"I like that," I say, and she smiles. Before I can stop myself, I add, "I like you."

She smiles up at me. "I like you too, and can I tell you what I'd like right now."

"Yeah."

"I'd like to see your cock."

Hearing sweet Josie use the word cock makes me smile. I like it. I like it a lot. "I'll show it to you. If that's what you really want."

"It is." She tugs her bottom lip between her teeth as I tear into my pants and shorts, kick them to the floor, and free my cock. I take it into my hand and her eyes widen.

"You good, Josie?"

"I...am."

"Good. Do you want me to tell you what I'd like right now?"

She puts her hand up, palm out, to stop me from speaking and my heart stalls. Shit, did I fuck this up already? I let go of my cock, and it stays erect, pointing at the woman it wants, when she shimmies out of her pants, lays back on the bed, and spreads wide for me.

"Motherfucker," I whisper under my breath and her soft chuckle curls around me.

"I thought we'd get back to the showing instead of telling."

I stare at her hot pinkness, her wet folds glistening in the overhead light. My cock jumps and I take it back into my hand. "It is. Show me everything," I command in a soft voice.

She slides her hands down her body and parts her lips, offering herself up to me completely and I growl, forcing myself to think about something, anything—high school math, taxes, my next game—to keep myself from shooting a load off simply from looking at her. Yeah, that's how much I want her.

"Did you need something?" I ask, some stupid part of me wanting to hear her say she needs me, wanting her to describe all the delicious things I plan to do to her.

"I need your mouth between my legs, Brody. I need to..." She takes a deep breath, and lightly strokes her clit. "...feel."

She doesn't have to ask me twice. I climb onto the bed, slide my hands under her ass and lift her sweet, delicious pussy to my mouth for a feast, and feast, I do. I press my mouth against her, eat like a man starved, my tongue all over her, in her, until she's gripping the sheets and chanting my name. I fucking love it.

I change the pressure of my tongue, slide it over her clit as I shift and dip one finger into her hot core. Her muscles instantly clench around me and I swear to God, the second I put my cock into her I'm a goner. So fucking wet hot and tight. I'll never last, and I damn well know it.

"Brody...I'm..." Her words fall off and I no longer think she's breathing. I tilt my head to see her, and she's still, her eyes closed as she hovers somewhere between heaven and earth. Her pussy clenches hard around my fingers, followed by a rush of warmth, her sweet release dripping down my hand. I refocus and lap at her, drinking in every drop of her sweetness as she rides out each powerful wave. Something inside me swells, something I can only call pride. I love that she opened to me, gave herself over to me and I was able to bring her these moments of bliss where the world disappears and nothing but pleasure matters. It's an honor.

Her body settles and I lift my head and find her up on her elbows, her eyes glossy as she gazes at me. "Hey," I whisper. She smiles, and reaches for me. "Something you want?" I tease.

"Yes. I want you to put your cock in me. Isn't that exactly how you described what we were going to do?"

"Such a dirty talker, Josie."

"Oh, you like that, do you?" she says with a soft chuckle.

"Maybe I do."

"Maybe you'll like this too."

Before I even realize what she's doing, she shoves me, hard—how does someone so little have so much strength?—and I'm flat on my back.

I gaze up at her as she shimmies on the bed, offering me a perfect view of her sweet, heart-shaped ass. "What are you doing?" I manage to get past a tight throat.

"I want to taste you. It's only fair. You got to taste me."

Even though I'm anxious to get inside her, the second she takes my cock into her small hand, the protest falls from my lips. "Josie..."

With her other hand, she pushes my shirt up to expose my stomach, and I grip it and rip it off until I'm naked too. "That's better," she says, running her fingers over my abs. "And wow, you are cut."

I grin, a little sheepish but loving the compliment. I'm glad she likes what she sees. But I can't think about that right now. Nope, not when she's lowering her head and taking my thick cock into her hot mouth. Her lips stretch around me, and I grab her hair to hold it away from her face. I don't want to miss a second of the action. The truth is, watching her suck me is the hottest thing I've ever fucking seen, and I should probably stop watching and think about my taxes again, because yeah, I'm that fucking weak at the moment.

Dude, you are so fucked...in more ways than one.

10

JOSIE

He quivers beneath my touch and that sends sparks of satisfaction racing through me. I was worried about pleasing him. I know what it's like for these hockey players, the hot girls who follow them around. That worry was for nothing, and honestly, it's nice to *feel* again, but more than that, it's nice to share this with Brody. I love experiencing his reactions to my...reawakening. Is that what I'm calling it? I guess in a sense it is, considering I haven't felt a man's hands on my body in a very long time. And you know what? I wouldn't want it to be any other man's hands on me, inside me. Brody's words, his touch, everything about him reassures me and gives me the freedom to let go, to just forget about real life for a while.

I take him deep into my throat and his growls and low curses curl around me and fill me with a new kind of need. Even though I just orgasmed, my sex is clenching again, looking for something to grip on to. I slide my hand between his legs and cup his balls. His hips lift as I caress him and when his cock hits the back of my throat, cutting off my oxygen, I choke a little. I don't care, though. I'm ready to take him even deeper when he grips my shoulders and eases me off him.

I'm about to tell him I'm okay, until my eyes meet his. My breath catches. Never in my life have I seen a man look at me with such intensity. "Brody..." I whisper.

"You have to stop." His voice is low and tortured. "Josie, baby, I'm right there. You have to stop. If you don't, I'm going to come down your throat."

"Maybe I like that idea."

He exhales sharply and briefly shuts his eyes like that image is playing out in his mind. "Yes, I want that too. I want that so fucking much, but the first time with you, I want to be inside you."

"I want that too, Brody." I move, and lay flat on my back. I bend my legs, put my hands on my knees and spread myself wide open. "Condom?" I ask. His gaze is latched on my pussy and I slide my hand down and lightly touch myself.

"Brody?"

"Huh?"

"Condom," I repeat as his gaze moves to mine, my words clearly not registering. "If you want to fuck me, we'll need a condom."

He blinks, coming out of some trance he was in, and blurts out, "Right." Jumping from the bed, he grabs his pants. He roots out a condom and I try really hard not to think about how fast he produced one, or how he keeps them at the ready. This is not about his past, or mine, or anything else. This is just about two people, having fun.

He tears into it and sheathes himself. I reach for him and he moves between my legs. He puts his hands on my knees, and holds me as his cock hovers around my opening. He moves his hips and I groan as he brushes against my clit, my body warming all over again. I don't usually come twice during sex, but everything about this is unusual.

I move my body, writhe and try to get him inside me. He reaches between my legs, takes his cock into his hand and presses it against me. "You want this?" he asks.

My eyes practically roll back in my head as his crown stretches me. "Yesss..."

His hips move, stretching me a little more and stupid tears press against the back of my eyes. I honestly didn't expect this to mess with my emotions. But all the fun we've been having, the tree in my living room...Brody in my bed. It's all hitting at the same time.

His hand lands on my cheek, and I blink up at him, take in the tenderness in his gaze as he looks back. Does he know I'm fighting to stave off the deeper things he's making me feel? Or does he think I'm having a hard time since he's my first in a long time?

"Let me make you feel really good, Josie."

The way he looks at me, like bringing me pleasure is more important than his own, steals my ability to speak, so I nod in response. In one fast thrust, he's inside me, his crown hitting my core so hard and so beautifully, it sends sparks of pleasure through me.

"Yes," I cry out and put my hands around his neck as he falls over me, his mouth on mine. He kisses me deeply, stealing all my thoughts, until I can't think, only feel. I grip his hair, tug, and slide my legs around his ass to hang on for the ride.

His cock is thick inside me, gloriously stretching me, and I revel in his girth and hardness. I move, eager for him to fuck me. His hands move to my hips and his fingers press into me for leverage as he inches almost all the way out, only to slam back into me again.

"Ohmigod," I yell, and his mouth moves to my throat, his labored breaths hot against my skin as he wets my flesh with kisses. Our bodies move together, and his arms slide around me, hold me to him and my heart squeezes. It's been so long since I've been held like this, another bevy of emotions races through me and this time, I let them tug at my fragile heart.

I close my eyes and ride out each wave of bliss, my body tightening, preparing for another earth-shattering climax as Brody pumps into me. I race my hands over his hard back, desperate need to touch every inch of his skin, all his hard muscle pulls at me.

I moan. "Brody," I murmur, and slide my hands to the small of his back, following the motion of his hips as he pumps in and out of my body, each downward thrust stimulating my clit. I whimper with pleasure. "So good."

"I know, Josie. Believe me, I know."

I hug him to me, our bodies entwined, moist, as the world once again closes in on me. I can't believe I'm about to climax again.

"Jesus," he growls as my sex tightens around his pistoning cock, and his hands move up my back to grip my shoulders. His body curls into me, and I sense he's straining to hang on, but I don't want him too. I want him to feel, too.

"Come with me, Brody."

"Josie..."

"Let me feel you."

He nods and drives in once, twice, then stills high inside me as I continue to clench around him, wave after wave of pleasure surging through me until I'm completely lost in euphoria. His cock swells impossibly more, and he growls as he lets go.

"Ohmigod, yes," I say as he pumps into the condom and for one brief second I hate the barrier between us. Especially when we've both been so open and honest. I like that about Brody. Like that he doesn't keep secrets. Integrity is important to me.

He pulses and throbs and when he finally depletes himself, he collapses on top of me. "Josie," he murmurs, and bends his head to take my nipple into his mouth. He licks me gently as we both slowly come back from bliss, and when I slide my hands through his hair, his head lifts, his eyes meeting mine.

"That was...fun," I say with a small laugh.

"Yeah, it was," he agrees and presses his lips to mine for a slow, easy kiss that curls through my blood and wraps around my heart. "I like having naps with you."

That makes me laugh out loud. I stretch my arms, and yawn. I haven't had a day off in so long, it feels good just to relax and forget about real life for a while.

"We can still have that nap," I say.

"I like that idea."

He eases out of me, and my body feels so empty without him. Who knew he'd become an addiction so fast? He discards the condom, and I make a move to get up, to clean up, but his big hand splays over my chest and he holds me down.

"Stay here. Rest. I'll be right back." I lay on my pillow, and stark naked, he walks to my door, and I grin at his cute ass. Water runs in the bathroom and he comes back with a wet cloth to wash me down and a stupid, emotional lump pushes into my throat at his sweetness.

Once we're clean, we snuggle in and I put my cheek on his heart. My mind slows, my body so thoroughly pleasured, I begin to drift off, until a noise pulls me back. My bedroom door creaks open and a heavy weight lands at the foot of my bed.

"You forgot to close the door," I murmur. Miss Mabel snuck in. I lift my head, but he puts his hand around my neck and brings me back to his chest.

"I'm okay with it, if you are," he says, his voice groggy from sex. "But if she's not allowed in here, I'll put her in the other room."

My throat tightens even more. I've been independent for so long, I'd forgotten what it was like to have someone do things for you—because my needs are important to them.

Careful, Josie.

"I'm okay with it," I say and even though I'm working to keep my voice casual, a little bit of worry seeps in—worry that I could fall for this tough hockey player, a guy with a zest for life, a guy who is sweet and sensitive and puts my needs first. But maybe I'm wrong. Maybe he wants to put Mabel in the other room, not because he wants to do things for me, but because he cares about her training. His body shifts, and even though my eyes are closed, I can feel his drilling into me, like he can sense my unease. I sigh and slow my breathing, and while he likes honesty, I'm not about to tell him I might be falling for him.

He settles as I slow my breathing, to give the illusion that I'm almost asleep, and a measure of guilt niggles at me. It's best I keep all these crazy emotions to myself. Honestly, I'm probably feeling things simply because I haven't been with anyone in a long time. I'm sure I'd be riding a roller coaster of emotions with any guy who was my first after my husband.

Are you really sure about that, Josie?

I shut down that annoying inner voice and focus on Brody's steady breathing. The next thing I know, my eyes are opening, and the second memories rush back, I turn to find the other side of the bed empty. Well, not entirely empty. My phone is sitting there. I snatch it up and find a missed video call from home, as well as a text from Brody, letting me know I missed a call, and that he took Miss Mabel out for a run.

I sit up in bed and check the clock, mentally calculating what time it is back home. It's four in the afternoon our time, which means it's ten at night in Switzerland, and my folks will still be up, but I certainly don't want to video chat with them from my bed, stark naked.

My stomach grumbles as I wrap a sheet around me and pad to the bathroom. I turn on the shower and step inside, letting the hot spray soothe my body. I grin, aching in places that have been dormant for a long time, but it's a good ache. A welcome one. I lightly touch my nipples and they pucker.

I reach for the soap and the rumbling of Miss Mabel and Brody's footsteps pounding up the stairs brings a smile to my face. I wait a moment, hoping he'll discover I'm awake and in the shower, and sure enough, the second he steps into the bathroom and spots me behind the steamy glass he starts stripping.

I crack the door. "You're pretty presumptuous."

His grin is wide, playful...full of want, and it's crazy how much I want him too, after orgasming twice.

"Are you saying you don't want me to join you?"

"Not saying that at all." I slide the glass door open wider. "I'm just saying you're presumptuous."

"Come on, you know you love it."

I laugh at that, and step back as he joins me, his big body eating up the space and overwhelming me in the most delicious ways.

"Presumptuous and a big ego." He angles his head, like he's waiting for me to continue. "What?"

"That's it, you're going to stop there." I eye him and he playfully adds, "You're not going to tell me something else is big." He grips my hips and pulls me against his very erect cock.

I laugh and smack his chest. "You're unbelievable."

"In bed, you mean."

I can't help but laugh at his playfulness. "Okay, Brody. You have a big cock and you're a God among men in bed."

"Well, now that we've cleared that up," he says and spins me so fast, I gasp. "How about I show you I'm a God among men in the shower too."

"Yes please," I say and that makes him laugh. He shimmies close, and I love the feel of his warm naked body pressed against mine.

He puts his mouth close to my ear, and his hot breath on my neck brings on a shiver. "You're not cold, are you, being out from under the hot spray?"

"Not cold at all," I tell him.

"Well that's too bad," he murmurs. "I was hoping to warm you up."

"Now that I think about it, there is a chill in the air."

"Atta girl." He slides his hands around my body, and cups my chest, then he goes still.

"What?"

"Shit. Your parents video messaged. Did you see that? I meant to ask you but you know, you naked in the shower. Kind of slipped my mind. Not much blood left there."

I wiggle my ass. "While I appreciate your concern, I'm not really interested in talking about my parents."

"Everything's okay though, right? It's not unusual for them to video message like that?"

I turn to him and cup his cheeks. "It's not usual." I go up on my tiptoes and put my lips on his, giving him a soft, gentle kiss my heart bursting from his sweet concern. I gesture with a nod. "If you're really worried, I can go—"

"Hell no," he says and I laugh, a bubble of happiness bursting inside me as he turns me again. I put my hands on the wall and wiggle my ass.

"Now, where were we?"

"Shit."

"What now?" I ask and glance at him over my shoulder.

He reaches for the handle on the shower door, agony all over his face. "I need to get a condom."

I put my hand on his wet arm to stop him and his blue eyes brimming with need latch on mine. "How about you don't."

He goes completely still, his jaw tight. "Josie, I...I mean, we can't..."

"I'm on the pill." God, what am I doing? "It regulates my cycle," I say quickly. As he stares at me like he can't quite decide what to do, I give a shrug of my shoulders. "I kind of like the idea of us doing it without one." His chest rises and falls quickly, like he's having a very hard time wrapping his brain around my sudden rash decision to have unprotected sex. Although it's not totally unprotected. I am on the pill. "I'm sorry," I say, mentally beating myself for my rash stupidity. This is an affair. A guy like Brody doesn't have sex without condoms, doesn't trust that a woman is telling the truth when she says she's on the pill. I'm sure famous guys have to be careful about not getting trapped into something they never wanted. I give a hard shake of my head. "It's a bad idea, isn't it. I'm sorry—"

"It's not a bad idea, Josie."

My heart jumps. "It's not?"

"No, it's not, not if it's what you want."

"What about what you—"

"I want what you want. I want to give you everything you want."

"Why...Why is that?"

He takes a hard breath, and his chest expands. He goes quiet for a brief second, like he's choosing his next words very carefully. "Let's just say, I do." At that non-answer, I nod, and he continues with, "I want this, and I promise you from the bottom of my heart that I'm clean."

"I trust you," I murmur, as my brain and body warm to the idea. "I'm clean too, and I would never do anything to deceive you. I know you guys must have to worry about that."

His brow furrows as he frowns, and I can only guess he's remembering something that isn't pleasant, but I want to put the smile back on his face, so I slide my hand down and take his big cock into my hand. "Now, where were we?"

He growls, and takes me into his big protective arms and presses his lips to mine for a mind-numbing kiss as I stroke him from base to crown, and revel in the way he thickens in my palm.

"Jesus, I love the way you touch me," he groans as he breaks the kiss and puts his mouth on my neck, his hand sliding between my legs to stroke my aching clit.

"Yes," I groan.

"Were you touching yourself before I joined you?" he asks, and I grin, understanding he's playing a game.

"Was I not supposed to?"

He growls in my ear. "You couldn't wait for me, baby. You needed it so bad, you had to put your fingers in here." He slowly slides a finger into my slick core, and I lose my ability to breathe as he strokes the sensitive bundle inside me, while the heel of his hand presses against my clit.

"I couldn't wait," I murmur as his other hand slides around my body to lightly stroke down my back. His touch is tender and soft, and even though he's already been inside of me, and is about to again, the gentleness in his caress curls around me and takes our intimacy to a whole new level. "I woke up and you were gone, and my pussy was aching to be filled. That just wasn't fair, Brody."

"Jesus," he curses. "Not fair at all. It was my mistake. I won't let it happen again." Pre-cum drips from his slit as my story turns him on, and while I was open and honest with my late husband, we never really engaged in sexy bedroom banter before. I never even knew I liked it until now. "But tell me how hard it was for you."

Speaking of hard. I swear to God his cock just thickened another inch in my hand. I tug on him and his hips move, sliding in and out of my palm, and I love the way he fucks my hand like that.

"Well, I didn't know what to do." I groan like I was in total agony. "I was hot, and achy and had no idea when you would get back…"

"So you decided to take a shower to ease the ache and cool yourself down?"

"Oh no, Brody. Not at all." I let go of his rock-hard cock, and he growls and takes himself into his hands. I back up and his finger slides from my sex, leaving me empty and disappointed, but I really want to tease him, maybe even torture him a little. There's something about the way I get to him that fills me with pleasure.

"I came in here to use this." I remove the nozzle from the shower cradle, and adjust the spray, until it's a pulsating stream of heat.

"No fucking way," he says, his voice deep and tortured, and he starts working his cock harder.

I blink at him. "I didn't think you'd mind if I came in here and gave myself an orgasm while I was waiting for you."

He exhales sharply. "I don't mind. I'm just glad I made it back in time to watch."

I angle my head and feign surprise, and as I do I wonder what the hell is going on with me. I never act like this, all confident and sexy and playful, but I have to say, I like the side of me he brings out. It's fun.

"You do?"

"Yeah, I do," he growls. He glances at the nozzle, his body so taut I worry something might snap. "Show me, Josie. Show me how you make yourself come." His gaze lifts to mine and I'm sure I've never seen him so aroused, so serious. "But after this, your orgasms are all mine. I don't want you to have to work for anything. I am going to make you come so many goddamn times you're not going to be able to walk by Christmas."

I smile, loving that idea as I spread my legs and center the nozzle between my legs. The hot spray bursts over my aroused clit, and a moan slips from my mouth. The sound is followed by tortured curses coming from the man working his cock in front of me. I move the nozzle and run it around my clit until pleasure gathers, focuses. I close my eyes, my head back and concentrate as one hand closes over my breast and rubs my nipple.

"Fuck yeah," he grumbles, his touch traveling through my body. "That feel good, baby?"

"God, yes." I move my hips, rock gently into the spray, shocked that I still have the ability to stand. His hand leaves my breast and the second he puts a finger inside me, I break like a dam around him, my body giving in to the pleasure as hot cum mingles with the warm spray.

"You are so goddamn beautiful when you come," he says and I open my eyes to find him staring at me, the blue in his eyes a deeper, darker shade as he focuses in on me. He takes the nozzle from me, puts it back in the cradle and turns me until I'm facing the back of the shower. He puts my hands back on the wall and he widens my legs with his foot. I whimper as his cock slaps against my ass.

"Brody," I cry out, and he doesn't make me wait, doesn't make me beg for what I need. Instead, he slides into me in one hard thrust and I scratch at the wall as he completely, beautifully fills me. It's crazy how much I needed this, needed him.

One hand goes around my waist to hold me, the other on my back, keeping me bent forward as he pulls out and slams back in again, taking as much as he's giving. His skin is hot against mine, no barriers to separate our flesh, which makes this hotter, sexier.

"You are so hot and tight, I'm not going to last."

"You don't have to last, Brody. We can do it again later. All night, in fact. I don't have anywhere else to be."

"Good, because there's nowhere else in the entire world I'd rather be than inside you."

My heart misses a beat at the way he makes me feel important, cherished. This guy could be with any woman he chooses and it's me he wants.

Don't let that go to your head, girl. This is just sex. Great sex, but sex nonetheless.

His other arm goes around my waist, and he reaches down to stroke my clit, and much to my surprise the third orgasm of the day hits, and as I soak his cock with my hot juices, he slams high and deep, hugs me tighter and spills his seed in me.

"I feel you," I cry out, as emotions clog my throat. Tears threaten as he fills me, not just my body, but my heart too. I'd forgotten how nice it was to be touched, to be held. Brody is doing crazy things to my body, my heart and my soul.

He presses kisses to my back as he continues to pump me full of his seed, and I love that we have nothing separating us, and that when he drips out of me later, it will bring a smile to my face and take me back to this exact moment.

He pants hard, and his warm breath sends shivers down my spine. He mistakes it for being cold, and with his cock still inside me, he tugs me until I'm upright. He backs us up until the warm water is on us and we both stand there in silence, lost in our own thoughts as we come down from our high.

He moves my wet hair from my neck and kisses my shoulder. "How do you feel?" he asks, breaking the quiet as the water starts to cool. Not sure I can—or should—put into words what I'm really feeling, I move and he slides from my body. I turn to face him, the smile on my mouth telling him all he needs to know.

He chuckles, and brushes the back of his knuckles over my flushed cheek. "Same." Warm lips find mind for a tender kiss. "How about we get out of here, and I'll make us something to eat."

"Okay," I say lazily, dreamily.

"Or do you want me to carry you back to bed?"

"Okay," I say again and he just laughs.

His eyes widen. "Wait, you have to call your parents."

My heart skips a beat. I love that he's so worried about me talking with my parents. I guess my relationship with them means a lot to him, knowing he's never had much of a relationship with his own.

"Dressed. First."

He laughs. "You go to your room, get dressed, and call your parents. I'll go make us something to eat."

"Okay."

He turns off the water, ties a towel around his waist and wraps me up in one. He lifts me and carries me down the hall. "You know, I kind of like that I can reduce you to one word answers."

I laugh and he sets me on the bed, and I take a few breaths to refill my brain. He walks to my door and my gaze goes to his strong back.

"Thanks."

He grins at me. "You're thanking me for sex?"

I smile. In a sense, yes, but this is so much more than sex to me. This is me living again. "I'm thanking you for...everything."

"Anytime, babe."

I laugh as he leaves and the sounds of pots and pans snap me back to reality. I dress quickly, and grab my tablet. I quickly check the time, and knowing they'll be up, I hit video call. My Mom answers with a smile on her face and she calls Dad over.

"Darling, how are you?" Mom asks.

"Great, Mom, missing you all."

She frowns. "I hate that you're spending Christmas alone."

A movement at the door catches my eyes, and I spot Brody there, Mabel at his feet, and I frown. "What?"

"Can I say hello?"

Panic races through me. Why the heck would he want to say hello to my parents and what are they going to think. It was only last year I lost Jon. What will they think of me?

"Is someone there with you, dear?" Dad asks.

"Uh, yeah. A friend." I glance up and take in Brody's smile. "He wants to say hello, is that okay?"

Mom and Dad exchange a look I don't quite understand. "By all means," Mom says when she turns back to me.

Brody plops down on the edge of my bed, his outer thigh brushing mine and sending tingles through my body. "Hi there."

They both go silent, and I worry I made a big mistake. They think it's too soon for me, and of course they're right. I shouldn't be sleeping with Brody, shouldn't have invited him to stay with me and I sure as hell shouldn't have let him video message with my parents.

"Mom—" I begin and I'm about to end the call, when Dad speaks.

"You're Brody Tucker, from the Seattle Shooters."

My heart starts racing. Okay, now I get it. They're star-struck!

"Yeah, it's me," Brody says.

"Brody this is my Mom and Dad, Elias and Astrid Larsson."

"Nice to meet you both. It's a shame you can't all be together for Christmas, but don't worry I'm here and I'm going to make sure Josie has a fantastic holiday season. Wait until you see the tree. Although, it will actually have to wait. We haven't decorated it yet."

I sit here with my jaw open as he talks to my parents, putting them at ease, like they've been friends for ever. Mom and Dad smile and move a little closer to the screen, and I suddenly feel like a bug under a microscope.

"Josie, you didn't tell us you knew Brody Tucker."

"Just Brody, sir."

My dad smiles. "Brody it is, and you can call us Elias and Astrid."

"Nice to finally meet you both. I'm looking forward to getting to know you better."

I stare at him, my jaw on my lap. What the hell is he doing? We don't have to pretend to be a couple in front of my parents. Which begs the question, what the hell is he doing?

BRODY

T hree days until Christmas Eve:

Despite it being early Monday morning—did all these people miss the memo that Mondays suck?—the streets are busy, alive with activity as I finish walking Mabel and head toward home. Technically it's not my *home*, it's Josie's place, yet in the few short days I've been staying with her, it's somehow started to feel like my home too, and I haven't been this happy on a Monday morning in a very long time. But I can't think like that. We're just having fun, right? Nothing more. All that sex was just...sex. Nothing deeper, no hidden meaning behind her touch, no telegraphed messages that she too might want more. Like I do. But will I fuck it all up in the end? The last thing I want to do is hurt Josie in any way. In fact, I want to do things for her, be there for her. With that thought in mind, I walk past the pharmacy, and see a photo kiosk where you can print pictures in minutes.

I tug my phone from my pocket, and grin as an idea forms. I open the door to allow Miss Mabel to enter, and she happily walks inside. I follow behind and a burst of warmth washes over me. I'm glad all the shops in this town are dog friendly and don't mind Miss Mabel tagging along. Chatter reaches my ear and I turn to find a bustling giftware boutique at one end of the store. The shelves are filled with unique Christmas gifts that customers are sorting through, and filling their baskets with last minute presents.

With Mabel in tow, everyone stops to pet her. People are so damn friendly in this festive town. I chat with a few people, and everyone asks about Josie. I like that they do, like that they care about her, and don't just want to know about me and my NHL career. It's clear that everyone now knows we're a couple, now. It's also clear how well liked she is in this small town. Then again, what's not to like? She's kind, and sweet and nice to everyone, except if you soak her with cold slush. I chuckle silently at that. She was having a bad day, and I made it worse. Guilt niggles at me as I think about her phone. I took a shit load of pictures of Mabel at the park today, and I really hope she had all her photos backed up. I would never forgive myself if she lost anything important.

I snatch up a cute picture frame that says, 'Best Pawent' and head to the kiosk to print some pictures. After we pay, we walk back home and Miss Mabel makes a beeline to her bed to collapse, all tuckered out from our play. I remove the frame from the bag and slide the picture in. Glancing around her place, I look for the best location to display the gift, and decide the perfect place is on the window ledge over the sink. It's the best place for her to notice it when she comes home and I hope it brings a smile to her face. Her place is in need of pictures. That thought makes me laugh, because my house is no different. It lacks warmth.

I send a text off to Declan to see what he's up to today, and head downstairs to the Chocolate Lab to check in with Josie. I reach the bottom step and look through the glass partition to spot Josie at the front counter, the phone pressed to her ear, panic all over her face. My heart leaps with worry, just as a noise in the lab catches my attention, and I turn to see Kayley. She smiles at me, but she too looks a bit frazzled.

"What's going on? Is everything okay?" I ask Kayley as she refills a tray with chocolate bark from one of the fridges.

"Our driver is out sick. We have a ton of orders and neither of us can go because we're too busy." I look through the partition again and count at least fifteen people milling about the store. Without thinking twice about it, I head back upstairs, grab my coat and hat and hurry back downstairs.

Josie's face lights up when she sees me, and it wraps around my heart and squeezes tight. "How did you and Miss Mabel make out?" she asks as she rings in an order. To the left of her, I spot boxes and bags with addresses on them.

"Great. She's napping."

"Are you going somewhere?" She glances at my head as I tug on my hat. "Hanging out with Declan?"

"Nope." I pick up one of the bags and check the address. "I'm headed to Acorn Street." She goes completely still, confusion on her face. "House number twenty-four, to be exact."

She turns from me and smiles as she bags the chocolate she just rang in and hands it over to the customer. "What are you talking about?" Her frown is back as she turns back to me.

I almost want to come back with a smart-ass comment, as I normally would, but she doesn't look like she's in the mood for teasing. "Kayley said your driver is sick, and I just happen to be free, and I have a car."

"No, Brody." She shakes her head and takes the box of chocolate from the next person in line. "I can't ask you to do that. You're here on vacation. I'll find someone."

"You already have."

As soon as the words leave my mouth, her gaze flies to mine. *You already have*. My God, I want to be the guy she finds, the guy she trusts not only her body with but her heart, too. Yes, I get it, she's a little lost, hasn't lived life in a long time, and is likely too afraid to put her heart on the line again after losing her husband. I don't blame her, but if she ever trusted me with it, I would be damn sure to treasure it. Damn sure not to do anything to fuck this up. I can't. I won't.

I gesture with a nod over her head. "Do you have any more out back, or is this it?"

"Brody, you don't have to."

"I want to."

"I can pay you."

"Oh, you'll pay," I say and give her a teasing wink. A blush crawls up her neck, and she nibbles her bottom lip like she's remembering all the fun we had last night. I turn to Kayley, who is grinning at the two of us. "Is this it?"

"For now," she tells me. "I'm sure there will be more when you return from this run."

I load up the bags, and the lady at the cash leans in and says to Josie, "You've got a good one there."

"Yeah, I do," Josie says and I toss a grin over my shoulders at her.

I head outside, and load the back of my car. I hop in and turn on the wipers to brush away the light dusting of snow. Off in the distance, I can see the ski hill. While I haven't quite made it there yet, I'm not disappointed. I'd rather spend every waking moment, and sleeping ones, with Josie and Mabel.

I jack the tunes, a strange new lightness inside of me as I meander through the decorated downtown core and veer off onto the streets filled with lit up houses. The deliveries take a lot longer than expected. Not only do I have to use my phone to search for the addresses, because I don't know my way around, but at each house, I have to stop and talk and take pictures. It's fun surprising people, though. No one expects to find me on their doorstep delivering chocolate. Once I'm done, I head back to the shop to get the next batch of deliveries. I take a look at the addresses, and plug them into my phone. I look at the last package, and it says pharmacy. I plug in the address, but it doesn't show up.

"Where is West Haven?" I ask.

Josie cringes. "It's far. I'm so sorry. It's two towns over. I didn't even know they had a pharmacy in West Haven. It's such a small place, it barely shows up on a map." She stacks more boxes of chocolates on the shelf, and glances at me over her shoulder. "You don't have to take that one. I can do it after work."

"No, you can't."

She frowns. "Why not?"

"You have plans after work," I tell her.

"I do."

"Yeah, paying me back. My God, your memory is short."

She laughs and whacks me. I capture her hand and I don't care who is watching, or if she thinks this is for show, but I bring her hand to my mouth and kiss it, unable to get enough of her.

I load up and after I do the local deliveries, I head to West Haven, and slow as I go down main street, which is nothing but fields, and old farms in the background. I check the address on my phone, and glance at the numbers on the mailboxes. I finally find the place, and as I turn into the long driveway and read the welcome sign, a laugh bubbles up in my throat. Josie had it all wrong. This isn't a pharmacy. Not really. Okay, well... it sort of is. I park at the big old farmhouse beside numerous other vehicles, grab the bag and make my way to the front door. As snow crunches beneath my boots and the smell of freshly baked bread and chili reaches my nostrils. A motor revs in the distance, and I glance up to see numerous snowmobiles going up a hill.

I knock and laughter from the backyard reaches my ear as the door swings open and an elderly lady smiles up at me.

"Delivery from the Chocolate Lab," I say and hand the bag over.

"Thank you." The lines around her blue eyes crinkle as she smiles up at me. There's a warmth about her, a real kindness, and I'd like to think if I knew my grandmother, she'd be very much like the woman standing before me.

"What is this place?" I ask, and her smile widens.

"Come on, I'll show you."

I spend the next half hour walking the old farm, and the whole time, all I can think about is how much Josie, and Mabel, would love this. Once I've taken in the place, I hurry back to my car and check the time. With any luck, Josie will be closing up shop and I can scoop up her and Mabel and take them back to West Haven.

I park on the street and spot Patrick leaving. Since she said he's always the first in and last out, I'm hoping she's finished for the day. I hurry inside and Josie's head lifts as I enter. "Are you okay?"

"Yeah, are you done for the day?" I glance around, and take in the empty store.

She puts her hand on her hip. "Are you that anxious for payment?" There's a wicked gleam in her eyes, and I suspect she's just as anxious as I am to crawl back into bed, or the shower, but I have other things on my mind.

"Yes, but it will have to wait."

She angles her head. "Wait? You're saying you're not anxious to extract payment from me?"

"Of course I am, and I plan to extract over and over again," I tease. I check the time on my phone. "But that will have to wait. There's something I want to show you."

"Oh?"

I laugh. "Not that. Well, yeah, that, but later."

"What are you up to, Brody Tucker?"

I pull myself up to my full height, and say, "Six foot two, but come on, there's somewhere I want to take you."

She removes her apron and places it on the counter. "But...I just finished. I have to shower, and make dinner, and Mabel has been inside most of the day."

"How about this, you shower later, and I'll help you with that. But right now, let's grab Mabel and don't worry about food. I've got us covered."

"What are you up..." She lets her words fall off and shakes her head. "Six foot two, right. Fine, let's go, but you know I don't like surprises."

"You'll like this one," I tell her and pull her into my arms for a kiss. Our mouths linger, and when she exhales, I realize just how tired she is. "I'm sorry, Josie. We don't have to go. I didn't stop to think that you've worked your ass off all day."

Her hand touches my cheek. "You are the sweetest, and I want to go wherever it is you want to take me."

Oh, if she only knew.

"Okay, finish doing what you need to do here, and I'll grab Mabel."

"I love how much you like including her in everything."

"I'm such a great boyfriend," I tease. "Besides, I love Mabel as much as I..." I catch myself before I finish that sentence, and my heart crashes in my chest as Josie stares up at me, her eyes narrowed, intense, and I shoot up a silent prayer of thanks that I didn't blurt out that I loved her. The last thing I want to do is spill my guts and scare her off.

Love her?

Yeah, I'm afraid that just might be true. But that scares me so much. I take a breath to pull myself together.

"Are you okay?" she asks and puts her hand on my arm.

"Yes," I answer quickly. "I just mean I love Mabel. She's such a sweet dog."

She opens her mouth, her brows knitted together like she's working through something. She glances down, and when her eyes lift to mine again she says, "Okay, you head on up to get her and I'll be right behind you in a second."

I hurry up the stairs and Mabel barks at the sound of my footsteps. I swing open the door and grin. It's so nice to be greeted by someone who is truly happy to see you. Bending, I give her an ear rub and in return get a big wet tongue across the face. I wipe away the wetness with my sleeve.

"We need to work on your greetings, girl." I check her bowl, give her fresh water and some food. When I'm done, I turn to find Josie standing there, a huge smile on her face as she takes the frame off the window sill.

"Brody...you did this?"

"Yeah, do you like it?" God, I sound so needy.

"I love it." She smiles at me, and my heart thumps. "This was so sweet of you." She throws her arms around me. "Thank you."

"I spotted it at the pharmacy, and thought you'd like it. You don't have many pictures around."

She backs up, and goes thoughtful. "You're right, I don't. It's not that I don't want pictures. I just haven't really had the time."

I put my hand on her waist and tug her to me. "Did you lose photos when you lost your phone."

"No."

I exhale and under my breath say, "Thank God."

She crinkles her nose. "What?"

"Nothing, I'm just glad you didn't lose anything."

She turns but not before I catch the sadness in her eyes, and she mumbles, "I don't know if I'd say that."

"Josie?"

She tugs her coat from the closet and turns my way, a smile on her face. "Nothing, let's get out of here. I could use some fresh air after a crazy day."

My pulse drums in my throat, and I want to press, want to ask what she lost, but it's clear she doesn't want me to push when she leashes Mabel up and heads to the stairs. I follow behind, an uneasy knot in my stomach. Maybe I could leave her phone somewhere that she could find it. But that would be wrong and deceitful. I tug the door shut behind us and follow her down the stairs, my mind racing and searching for solutions.

After Mabel does her business, we all pile into the car, and Josie rests her head against the seat, a small smile on her face as she turns to me.

"Thanks for getting me out of the house." Her hand slides across the seat and she touches mine. "I'm looking forward to my surprise."

I start the car, and Mabel presses her nose to the window as I pull into traffic and head for the highway. Josie sits up a little straighter. "Where are we going?"

"Have you ever been to West Haven?"

"Actually, no." I nod, and feel her eyes on me. "You made out okay with your delivery there today?"

"Oh, yeah, for sure."

"Why are we going back?"

"You'll see."

She just shakes her head at me. "Fine, Brody. You can have your secrets."

She hums to the radio as I drive, and conversation turns to her parents and how much she misses everyone. As she reminisces, an idea forms. If she can't go home for Christmas, maybe I can bring home to her.

Soon enough, I pull off the highway and drive through the quaint town of West Haven. "So pretty here."

"They don't decorate quite as much as Holiday Peak, but close."

"Where's the pharmacy you delivered to today?"

"Right here," I say, and pull off the road. She stares straight ahead at the big old homestead in the distance, and the busy hill behind it, kids and adults both sliding down it on toboggans.

"What..."

I point to the sign. She reads it, and her nose crinkles. "Farmacy? I don't get it."

"It's not a pharmacy, it's a bed and breakfast, and they have tons of different animals that guests can pet for therapeutic healing. A farm-acy. It's brilliant."

Her jaw drops open. "No way."

"Yeah, and you don't have to stay at the bed and breakfast to do it. It's open to the public. I already bought us tickets, and they use the funds to care for the animals. They have snowmobiles, sleds, and all the animals we can pet."

Her smile is so big, it lights up her entire face. "I love this, Brody."

"I figured you would."

"Asking around about me again, were you?"

"Nope, don't need to. You're an animal lover, and after seeing the stress on your face today, I thought you could use a natural, therapeutic treatment to unwind. You're wrapped up in getting all your orders correct for others, but you can't forget about yourself."

"You won't let me do that."

"Damn right I won't." Mabel sticks her head between the seats.

"They won't mind Miss Mabel?"

"Dogs are welcome. I asked. They have an area where she can play with other dogs. She'll love it."

I slowly go up the driveway and park, noticing there are a few less cars than this afternoon. Josie hops from the car, and Mabel follows her out. She's spinning in circles with all the new smells. We leash her and head to the back of the house, where we're greeted and shown around. We introduce Mabel to the other dogs in the fenced off area and head to the barn for chili and fresh biscuits. I'm not sure I've ever seen Josie smile so hard.

"How did I not know about this place?" she asks as we sit at one of the large tables, and dig into our food.

"You haven't really lifted your head in a long time," I tell her, and give her thigh a little squeeze.

She tugs on my hat, and I take it off. She laughs at the mess of my hair, and says, "You're right, but I'm having fun now."

"Good. That's the main thing." I take a spoonful of chili. "This is so good."

We're joined by a young couple, and their daughter, who looks to be around four. We say hello after they introduce themselves as Brad and Talia, and their daughter, Madison, we introduce ourselves, and Brad's eyes bug out of his head.

"I thought that was you," Brad says, a big smile on his face. "What are you doing here?"

"Enjoying the farmacy with my girl, Josie."

"Honey," he says, "this is Brody Tucker from the Seattle Shooters."

Talia gives me an apologetic look. "I'm sorry. I don't follow sports."

"No worries," Josie says with a laugh. "I don't really either."

"Mommy, I want to go sledding," Madison says.

"We will. Right after we finish eating." She smooths her daughter's hair from her face, and I don't miss the way Josie is looking on with longing. Children were once a part of her future, and it's clear she still wants them.

"What's been your favorite part about the farm so far?" Josie asks, and Madison cradles her arms and rocks them like she's holding a baby.

"I love the little lamb. Mommy, can we take that lamb home?"

Talia rolls her eyes and laughs as she gives her daughter a hug, and I almost hear a wistful sound rise up in Josie's throat. "We'd have a whole farm if it was up to her."

"I can't wait to see and hold the baby lamb," Josie says.

"I'll show you how to do it," Madison says, a very serious expression on her face. "You have to be very careful. They're just babies, you know."

I bite back a laugh as the little girl jumps from five to fifteen right before my eyes. Or maybe that's normal. I've only ever been around my teammate's kids and not for long periods of time. I really don't know the first thing about being a parent. But it doesn't look so bad.

Josie grins. "I would love it if you showed me."

"Then we can race down the hill on our toboggans. Right, Mommy?"

Talia's expression turns apologetic again. "I'm sorry, you don't have to—"

"Oh no. I want to," Josie interrupts, as she leans into me, nudging me with her body. "Brody here might look like he's an adult, but he's really just a twelve-year-old boy at heart."

"Hey, I resemble that comment," I tease, and throw my arm around her. Her warmth wraps around me and squeezes tight, and laughter bubbles up inside me. My God, I love being with her. She's so fun, so easy.

Everyone laughs and Talia says, "If you're sure. I don't want to intrude upon your day. It's just that Madison here has never met a stranger." Her gaze goes back and forth between the two of us. "Do you two have kids?"

Josie opens her mouth but I pipe up. "Not yet." I pull Josie closer, and kiss her cheek. "But I'm always willing to work on it." I love the pink flush on Josie's cheeks and suspect I'll pay for that later. I'm looking forward to it.

Talia smiles at us. "You two are a very cute couple, and your kids will be gorgeous."

"Can we talk about hockey now?" Brad asks.

We all laugh and Talia nudges her husband. "Don't be rude. I'm sure Brody has better things to talk about."

"It's fine. I could talk hockey all day."

"Fine, you two talk hockey," Josie says. "I want to hear more about these farm animals. Can you tell me more, Madison?"

"Oh yes."

I laugh at Madison as she goes back into teenage mode. As the girls talk, Brad and I go over a few of the stellar plays made so far this season, and before we know it, we're all done eating and headed to the petting zoo.

We spend the next few hours petting the animals, racing our new friends down the hill, and taking a short snow mobile ride along the trails. By the time we're done, we're both exhausted. We say goodbye to our friends as Brad scoops up a very sleepy Madison, and we collect Miss Mabel, who has been playing in the snow.

We drag our feet as we head back to the car and once we're buckled in, Josie exhales and her head turns my way. "Thank you, Brody. I've had the best day ever."

"It's not over yet."

She stifles a yawn. "No?"

"There's this payment we need to talk about."

She chuckles. "Right, how could I forget about that."

"You're tired, so I'm going to make it easy on you."

"Really?"

"You can just lay there. I'll do all the work."

"That is awfully sweet of you."

"What can I say, I'm a damn good boyfriend."

"I am so lucky."

"Nah, I'm the lucky one," I tell her, and mean it from the bottom of my heart. The problem is, though, I want to be more than just her boyfriend.

I just have to figure out how to convince her she wants that, too.

JOSIE

Two days until Christmas Eve:

"It's a gorgeous day," I say as I step back into my loft after taking Mabel for an early morning walk. Last night Brody said he'd take her out and let me sleep in, but he was sleeping so peacefully I didn't have the heart to wake him, plus he's been doing so many things for us, it's only fair I take my own dog out for a walk. She's my responsibility, not his, and when he leaves, it will be back to just the two of us.

As soon as I realize Brody isn't in the kitchen, I wince, hoping I hadn't woken him. I figured he'd be up by now but no, the place is silent so he must still be sleeping. I unleash Mabel and press my finger to my lips, suggesting she be quiet, not that she can understand. Brody is the dog whisperer, not me. That brings a smile to my face but it falls fast. Mabel is going to miss him when he leaves.

I'm going to miss him when he leaves.

Damn. Damn. Damn.

I put on a pot of coffee, and ignore the sinking sensation in my gut. As it percolates, Brody's voice trickles down the hallway and reaches my ears. Is Brody talking to someone? I quietly walk down the hall and my foot hits the door, opening it an inch.

Brody's head lifts and pales as he glances at me. My gaze drops to take in my open tablet, balanced on his lap. He quickly shuts it.

"I didn't realize you were back." He rakes his fingers through his mess of hair, combing it in place. "You were so quiet."

I glance at my tablet as he slides it to the side like he's trying to hide it from me. "I thought you were still sleeping."

He stretches, and my gaze goes to his T-shirt as it pulls snug over his shoulders. "I just woke up. Checking...uh, the weather."

I've not known him long, but in the few days we've spent together, I never once got the sense that he was lying about something. Until now. "Why didn't you use your phone?" It's strange that he'd grab my tablet and not his phone, a device he's not only familiar with but was sitting right next to him. He had to get up to get my tablet from my dresser.

"I couldn't find it." He scratches his head and glances around.

"It's right there, on the nightstand."

He laughs, but it's a bit forced and shaky. "I guess I must still be half asleep. Saw your tablet and just grabbed it."

"What's it calling for?"

"What?" he asks quickly.

"You were checking the weather. What's today's forecast?"

"Oh." He shoots a glance at the window. "Nice and sunny."

I cross my arms and gaze at him. Why is he acting so cagey? "It's gorgeous out. Cold, but the sun is shining."

He pushes to his feet. "A nice day to do deliveries."

I shake my head. "You don't have to. Our driver is back today. Thank goodness."

His eyes light, clearly happy about that. Was yesterday a hardship? Did he not want to do deliveries? That can't be right. He pushed to help and he was so excited about finding the farmacy. But maybe he's tired of playing house. Maybe he's pushing away a bit because our time is almost finished here.

"Did you have plans?" I ask.

He nods quickly, steps toward me and drops a kiss onto my forehead. "Yeah, I...well, Declan. We should probably hang out today."

"You absolutely should." Maybe he really was checking the weather and I feel bad that I've been monopolizing all his time when he came here to enjoy the holidays with his friend. "Are you thinking of hitting the slopes? It's a beautiful day for it."

"Yeah, that's a good idea."

My gaze goes to my tablet again, and as much as I want to open it, check it, I also don't want to. I don't want to think he's being deceitful. What could he possibly be trying to hide from me? Heck, if he was hooking up with another girl, he sure as hell wouldn't be doing it on my tablet. I have to be making more out of this than it really is, and I can't forget that he's leaving here shortly. I should just enjoy this time while I can and not read anymore into his strange behavior.

"I should get going."

I gesture with a nod. "I need to get to work too. Coffee is on."

"How late do you think you'll have to work tonight?"

"I think most people have already picked up their candy for the holidays. I don't think it's going to be a late night at all." I turn, head to the kitchen and he follows me. Mabel finishes eating and he drops to his knees to pet her. "I'd better go," I say finding it hard to tear my gaze away from Brody as he pets Mabel, and wishing his hands were on me instead. It's crazy to think I'm jealous of my dog.

"Okay, see you later," he says and I note the way he's not looking up at me. I honestly have no idea why he's acting so strange.

I leave him with Mabel and head down to the shop, and as soon as I flip the sign and unlock the door, in walks Patrick with a fresh new haircut.

"Hey Patrick," I say. "I love the new haircut."

A sheepish look comes over his face. "My barber was out sick and I was desperate so I went to Chatters."

"I know lots of men that go to the hairdressers for a cut. Nothing wrong with that." I grab my apron and tie it around my waist, and glance past Patrick's shoulder to see Brody's car drive down the street. He sure is in a hurry to get to the slopes or wherever it is he's going.

Patrick walks up to the display window and picks out a few chocolates for his lunch break. "Is Brody enjoying Holiday Peak?" he asks.

"He sure is. We've been having a lot of fun." Honestly, last night at the Farmacy was so much fun. I do love his childlike enthusiasm and zest for life.

He nods. "You two make a nice couple."

"Thank you."

He looks away, a frown on his face, and I suspect he has something on his mind. Kayley comes in, and we both greet her. She goes to the back room to grab her apron and take the chocolate from the fridge.

"How are your holiday's going, Patrick?" I ask.

He shoves his hands into his pockets. "Good. Good." He nods, slowly walks around the store, takes a breath and in his most casual voice says, "Nikki cut my hair."

"She did a great job," I say.

"Yeah, she is," he agrees, and I don't miss the quirk in the corners of his lips. "I mean, yes she did a great job. Um...do you know if she and Declan are a couple. I know they're friends, but I was wondering if they were more than that."

"All I really know is that they're friends from childhood. Other than that..." I let my words fall off.

"Right, right," he says brushing it off. "Just curious."

Holy crap, Patrick likes Nikki. I honestly don't know what the deal is with her and Declan, but if Declan really likes her, he'd better let her know. Patrick is one of the good ones, and he lives in this town. He's also not known as the heartbreaker.

He might be a bit shy, a little awkward around women, but I think any woman would be lucky to have him. It's not my business and I don't like gossip, but maybe I should say something to Brody.

Kayley comes back in and answers the phone when it rings, and she takes today's orders as Patrick pays for his chocolates. The bell over the door jingles. I glance up quickly, some small part of me hoping Brody is back. But he's not. It's just a few customers.

"Enjoy those chocolates," I say to Patrick as he heads out into the early morning sunshine. The day passes quickly, more customers coming in than I'd expected. By the time lunch rolls around, I run up and grab Miss Mabel and take her for a walk. I scan the street for signs of Brody's car, but it's nowhere to be found. I glance at the ski hill and ignore the strange sensations in my gut—I don't want to think about how cagey he was earlier—and hope he's having a good time with his buddy, Declan. We make our way to Coffee Klatch.

I push open the door, and Miss Mabel goes crazy with the smells, but you know what she doesn't do? Jump or pull or try to steal anyone's treats.

"Good girl," I say and give her a pat on the head.

Mabel waves to us from behind the counter. "Hey stranger. I haven't seen much of you lately."

"Been crazy busy."

She eyes me. "Yes, you do have a flush on your face from all that work."

Oh, God. I am not going to discuss my sex life with her. We've talked about a lot, and she's been there for me since I've moved here, but sex talk is crossing a line.

"Brody has been doing a great job with Miss Mabel."

"He really has. He's been helping me with a lot of things."

"I bet he has," she says with a grin on her face. "He seems really nice."

"He is nice." Nice, and sweet and good with his hands, and mouth... Oh boy.

"You okay?" Mabel asks.

"Yeah, sure why."

"Oh, no reason. You drifted for a bit there."

She has the sweet, but know-it-all smile on her face. "Just thinking about all the orders I need to get out. Which means I'd better hurry. Could I grab a couple ham and cheese sandwiches and a couple coffees?"

"Sure thing, and we can't forget Miss Mabel's treat. What's the sense in living if we can't have a treat every now and then?"

I just nod, even though I suspect she's talking about Brody, and it's true, he's been a real treat, a big fat snack, in so many ways. I pay for our purchases, and head back outside. In the loft, I give Miss Mabel her treat, and try hard not to think about the treat who's been in my bed and how our time is coming to an end.

I hurry back downstairs, and after Kayley and I quickly eat, we get to work. I didn't call in any part time workers, thinking these last couple days would be slower, and while the afternoon dragged on, probably because I'm anxious to meet up with Brody, we were rather busy. I check the clock for the hundredth time, and wonder what Brody might like to do about dinner. He'll be ravenous after a day on the slopes, I'm sure. With only a half hour left, in saunters Declan and I glance past him, searching for Brody.

"Hey," I say to him. "How was skiing?"

He angles his head. "Skiing?"

I stiffen, but quickly try to brush off my alarm by waving my hand and saying, "Oh, nothing. I thought you and Brody were skiing today."

He goes still, and his brow furrows, like he's trying to figure out if he was supposed to be covering for his buddy. He pulls his phone from his pocket. "He did text me first thing this morning. I messaged him back that I was busy, and that was it. I guess he must have gone by himself. Yeah, I'm sure he did."

"Can I get something for you?" I ask and plaster on my best smile, like my insides are not on a roller coaster ride, wondering what Brody is doing and why he doesn't want me to know he's doing it. The truth is, though, he can do what he wants. He doesn't owe me an explanation and doesn't have to clear any of his actions with me first.

"I want to get a box of chocolate nips for my mother."

"She does love them."

He nods and I grab a box and place the delicate pieces of chocolate in. As he pays for it, my mind goes to Patrick. While I'd liked to tell him that Patrick is interested in Nikki, I'm not sure it's my place. I think it's best if Brody talk to him.

After he pays, he heads out, and my gaze follows him, looking for signs of Brody's car. Soon enough, Patrick is back, and after he leaves, Kayley follows him out and I close the shop.

My feet hurt by the time I head to the stairs leading to my loft and delicious—familiar—scents reach my nostrils.

What is going on?

I hurry up the stairs and when I open the door and find Brody standing over my stove, Mabel at his feet as he wipes his hands on one of my old aprons. My heart soars.

"What did you do?"

He spins, his eyes wide and Mabel's tail wags as she comes running to me. I pet her and Brody's gaze flies to the clock. "You're done early." He looks flustered, and a bit panicky.

I step up to him, and try to see around his body, but he blocks me. "What are you making?"

"Stop it. It's a surprise."

I catch scent of my favorite dishes from home, and the pieces of the puzzle start to fit together. "Brody, did you video chat with my parents this morning to find out what my favorite foods were?"

"Maybe," he says, non-committal. "Maybe not."

That's what he was doing with my tablet. How incredibly sneaky and sweet of him. I throw my arms around his shoulders. "This...this is what you've been up to all day? Ohmigod, I can't believe it."

He picks me up, and kisses the top of my head. "Wait, what did you think I was up to?"

He sets me down and glances at me. "I thought you were skiing with Declan, but then he showed up at the shop."

"If you must know. I drove to three towns to find the perfect fondue pot and get the ingredients to make you this meal.

Now why don't you sit down and I'll pour you a glass of wine."

My heart thumps hard in my chest as I take a seat, and call Mabel over, but she's not about to leave Brody's side, not when he keeps feeding her cheese. "Why did you go through all this trouble?"

"It's no trouble at all, and I could tell how much you missed your family and I thought if you can't go to them, I could at least bring a piece of home to you."

"Brody, you're so—"

"Sweet, I know, I know." He gives me a playful wink. "Just doing what any good boyfriend would do."

"I don't know about that," I say as he hands me a glass of merlot.

"If a guy isn't doing things like this for you, Josie, maybe he's not the guy."

I chuckle, but it holds no humor, because I'm not sure there's a guy out there who could compare to Brody, who is only pretending to be my boyfriend. He sets the fondue pot on top of the brass holder, a candle lit underneath, and puts a tray of cubed bread beside it.

"Carbs, mmm, my favorite."

He removes his apron, and takes a sip of wine, and I watch him, realizing I could simply stare at him all day long and never get bored. He sits, and pokes the bread cube with the skewer, coats it in cheese and brings it to my mouth. I take a hearty bite and moan as my eyes roll back in my head.

"I haven't had this in so long, Brody. It's so good."

"If you moan like that again," he begins through clenched teeth. "I'll be abandoning this whole surprise and taking you straight to your bed."

I laugh at that. "While I like the idea of that, you spent too much time and effort for us to let this go to waste." I lean into him. "But when we're done, I promise to moan for you just like that, if you want."

He briefly closes his eyes. "I want. I want a lot, and you know, I think tonight I might just break the world record for the fastest eater." I laugh as he jumps up and plates saffron risotto with shrimp. "Your mom said this is traditionally served with luganighe, or as we like to call it here, sausage." He grins. "But I couldn't find any traditional luganighe and she said you liked it with shrimp, so prawns it is."

"It's perfect."

"You might want to save judgment until you try. This was my first time making risotto."

I slide my fork into the dish and take a generous bite. Unable to help myself, I moan around the delicious flavors, and Brody's growl mingles with the sounds.

"Oops sorry," I murmur, not at all sorry. It's fun to torture him, to know I can turn him on from a simple sound. I take another forkful and bite into it, another moan filling the air, and Brody's eyes narrow in on me.

"You're definitely going to pay for that."

I grin, because I can't wait.

BRODY

 ne day until Christmas Eve:

The last few days with Josie have been the happiest days of my life. When we weren't in bed together, we were snowmobiling, sledding, enjoying the Farmacy, working to fulfill chocolate orders, or sitting around the tree, watching Christmas movies, where tears might or might not have surfaced. I grin at her now as we finish eating leftovers at her small kitchen table, and I can't remember what my life was like before she came into it.

Light from the tree in the living room bounces off the walls and adds a shimmer of warmth and coziness to her kitchen as Josie takes her last bite of leftover risotto and exhales, a small smile on her face. She tugs on her yoga pants. "If I keep eating like this, I'm going to roll into the new year."

I laugh at that. "Stop it, you're perfect."

Her smile falls, and her brows pinch together, her mood doing a complete one-eighty. "Brody, when do you leave?"

"We were thinking the day after Christmas, but I'm thinking I might stay a bit longer."

"Really?" Her eyes light up.

"It depends," I say and set my spoon down.

She toys with her napkin. "On what?"

"If you let me kiss you when the ball drops."

"You can kiss me," she says, her voice low, almost a whisper as another change comes over her. She pushes back in her chair, and I don't just feel the physical distance, I feel the emotional one as well. Is she trying to put a chasm between us so she doesn't get hurt? Or is she just not ready to commit to more with me? The fact is, we've grown close, extremely close in a short period of time, and even though she's been happy—has been living again—the fact of the matter is, I have to leave. I've never been into long distance relationships before. Heck, I've never been into relationships. I want things now that I've never wanted before.

"Josie?"

She wipes her mouth with a napkin, her dark eyes wide when they meet mine. "Yeah."

"Can I ask you something?"

Her lips tighten, and she inches back in the chair more, and I know it's my imagination, but the temperature in the room seems to have dropped a few degrees. "Sure."

"Do you...um....us." I take a breath to pull myself together. "What are you doing tomorrow, for Christmas Eve?"

"Oh," she says, a measure of relief in her voice. What, was she worried I was going to ask for more, and she wasn't ready to give it? She said she wanted to start living life again, but that doesn't mean she's ready to give her heart to another man. It could very well still, and always, belong to her late husband.

She waves her hand toward her stove. "I was just going to bake, and sit around the tree."

"Do you think maybe you'd like to go to Declan's with me? His parents put on a big Christmas Eve dinner every year. I'm expected to be there, but I don't want to go unless you go with me."

A smile touches her mouth, and she inches back toward the table. "I think that would be nice." She picks up her plate. "What should I bring?"

"Damn, I never thought of that. I'll have to make a quick trip to the stores tomorrow to pick something up."

There's a new twinkle in her eyes when she smiles at me. "I have a better idea."

"Oh?"

She sets her dish in the sink, and I put mine in with it. "Come with me." Without putting our winter coats on, she leads me to her door, but I quickly realize we're not going outside, we're going to her store downstairs. It's quiet this time of night, all the shoppers are home, and the staff finished their workday.

"You're thinking a box of chocolates or something."

"Or something," she jokes, and takes me to the back room, where the big machines are set up and all the magic happens.

"I thought we could make a batch of fresh bark. It's my favorite, and I thought maybe you'd like to see the process."

"Yeah, I would."

"You sure it won't bore you?"

"Nothing you do can bore me, Josie." She smiles, but I'm not lying. I'm really interested in what she does, and it's easy to tell how much she likes it by the way she lights up whenever she walks into her 'lab.' "But you'll have to watch our next game."

"I already planned on it. Now I have someone else to watch besides Declan." My chest expands at the thoughts of her watching me, as she moves around the room, pointing out her massive amount of equipment. I listen intently, amazed by her knowledge and fascinated as she explains the process for the different kinds of chocolates she makes.

"For the bark, we have to use tempered chocolate, which I have here, otherwise the bark won't have a smooth glossy sheen and a crisp snap, and tempered chocolate won't turn dull and fuzzy if stored for a while."

"Tempered?"

She ties an apron around her waist and rolls up the sleeves on her sweater. "When chocolate is melted, the molecules of fat separate. Tempering brings them back together, and if done properly, you get a network of stable crystals. That's what makes it glossy, with a crisp snap."

I scratch my head. "I didn't realize I was going to get a science lesson. Can you say that again, using shorter sentences and smaller words?"

She laughs at me. "How about I show you instead?" She grins at me, throwing my words back at me, and my body reacts, wanting her in my arms again.

"You know I do prefer show over tell."

Grinning, she fills a pot with water and puts a bowl over it. "Today, we're only going to melt it, and this is how I like to do it, so it doesn't burn."

"I didn't even know you could burn chocolate."

"Grab me those bars over there," she says, and points. I walk over to a table, and lift the parchment paper to find rows and rows of chocolate. The rich cocoa scent fills my senses. "Can't we just eat this?" I break off a couple bars of chocolate and hand them to her.

"Trust me, the bark will be much better." She gestures with a nod as she turns the stove on and puts the bark in the bowl. "Go over to that fridge, and pick out the ingredients you might want in your bark."

I open the fridge to find peanuts, coconut, cranberries, peppermint and every kind of candy under the sun. "I think I've just died and gone to heaven." I grab a mixture and carry it to her. "Can we put all this stuff into one batch? Wait. Do we have any popcorn left? I bet the sweet and salty would be amazing."

Her jaw drops. "Are you kidding me?"

"About what?"

"Popcorn is my number one favorite thing to add to the chocolate. I don't have it on the shelves because it doesn't store well, but I make it for myself sometimes."

"It's almost like I know you."

She angles her head and eyes me suspiciously. "How did you know that?"

"I didn't."

"Did you ask my parents?"

"No, I just thought it would be delicious." She goes quiet for a second, lost in thought as she stirs.

"Hey, was it something I said?"

She shakes herself from whatever it was she was thinking. "Why don't you run upstairs and nuke a bag of popcorn for our bark which we can eat during movie time."

My heart jumps. I love that our evenings have become our movie time. "I'm on it." I hurry upstairs, greet a happy Mabel, who quickly begins to drool over the popping corn. I give her a handful and hurry back downstairs.

"All set," I say and shove a mouthful of popcorn into my mouth.

"Perfect time. Here, you stir." She holds the spoon up for me.

"I think we'll do peppermint bark for the Bradbury family. It's one of my biggest selling items this year. I can barely keep it on the shelf."

I take the wooden spoon from her and for a moment our hands touch, linger, and despite the physical distance she seemed to put between us earlier, neither of us are in a hurry to move.

"Get stirring before it clumps."

"Right." I drag my hand from hers, and stir the chocolate as she takes her new phone from her pocket and puts on some Christmas music. I want to tell her about her phone, but what good could come from that now? We've been having so much fun, and I don't want to do anything to ruin that. None of that helps with the guilt lingering in my gut, though.

She hums along to the music as she puts the candy cane between parchment paper and breaks it apart. I continue to stir as she holds a piece of candy out to me. "Open." I do as she asks, and she places a big piece on my tongue.

"Delicious. Did you make the candy cane, too?"

"Of course, I do. Other than the nuts and some of the packaged candy in the fridge, everything is homemade."

"You're a woman of many talents." She smiles at the compliment and leans over me to check the chocolate.

"Looking good." She dips a spoon in to taste it. "Almost there."

"What's next?"

She runs her hand over a big marble tabletop. "Once that's melted, I'll get you to pour the chocolate out onto the table, but you'll have to work fast. It needs to be smoothed out when it's still warm."

"I have a better idea. You're the chocolatier, how about you work your magic and I'll watch." Truthfully, I like learning new things, but it's more fun watching her. In fact, I would watch this woman all day and night and never be bored.

"That might be best for your first time, and we do want the bark perfect if we're giving it as a gift." It's crazy, but her using the word 'we' like we're a real couple, bringing a joint gift to a party, does the weirdest things to my insides. Good things, like warmth and happiness. Things I never want to stop feeling. She checks the chocolate again. "You better let me in there."

I hand her the spoon. "It's all yours."

I'm all yours.

Those words sit on the tip of my tongue as she pours the chocolate and grabs a spatula, quickly working and smoothing the chocolate like a pro. She hums along, lost in her work and I lean against the counter and admire her as she sways back and forth, and when she discards the bowl, I dip my finger in for a taste.

"Delicious," I say, thinking about all the fun things we could do with all the warm, gooey chocolate.

"Okay, Brody, go ahead and start sprinkling the candy cane, try to get it even and all over."

I grab a handful and start sprinkling, and she smooths the chocolate around the candy, our movements in sync. "What a team we are."

She pokes me with her elbow. "You're pretty good in the kitchen."

"I've got moves," I tease.

She chuckles, and I go to reach for more candy, but she stops me. "I think it looks perfect." Hands on hips, she steps back to admire her handiwork.

"Totally perfect," I say.

"We have to let this cool before we crack it, and that's the fun part."

"I think it was all fun," I say as she drops a bar of fresh chocolate into the bowl and puts it over the warm water.

She stirs the chocolate and my heart squeezes tight. I know we're playing house, but dammit, I want more. I want everything with this woman. Never in my life have I felt this way, or allowed myself to. I closed myself off, too afraid of loss and the hurt that comes with it. I'm not sure what's come over me. Maybe it's this town, the decorations, the holiday spirit, and the magic of Christmas all combined that makes me want to try out a real relationship with Josie. Heck, maybe it's none of those things, but it's simply sweet Josie herself who has faced so much—alone—and her strength has given me the courage to face my own fears of abandonment. I really don't know the answer to anything anymore, but what I do know is that I want to do better, I want to overcome the past and walk into the future with this incredible woman by my side.

But what does she want?

I touch her hair, brush it from her shoulder and she takes a fast breath. I'd have to be a fool not to realize the effect we have on each other, the chemistry arcing between us, but I get it. She's had loss, too, but if there is one thing this week taught me, it's that she *does* want to live again, but she's afraid of dishonoring her late husband's memory. Fate had to have brought us together for a reason, right? Was it so that we could start something new together, and help each other move forward?

As that thought settles in my brain, a warmth falls over me, a sense of contentment like I've never felt before encompasses my entire body. Now that I know what I want, I just have to convince her to see things my way, and show her that moving beyond a pretend relationship is the reason we were brought together, and that she deserves a future filled with happiness. To begin with, I have to come clean about her phone, and tell her I'm the one who found it. I don't want any lies between us.

Just don't mess this up, Brody.

Before the chocolate gets too hot, I dip my finger into the bowl, and brush it over her cheek.

"Hey, what do you think you're doing?" Instead of answering, I do it again, covering her chin and neck. "Brody!"

She lifts her spoon and flicks it at me, covering my face and hair, and we both laugh. I take the spoon from her, dip it into the bowl and flick it at her. She gasps and rubs the chocolate from her cheeks, smearing it more. I pull her to me, and press my lips to hers. I break the kiss and grin when I see our artwork.

"You're a mess."

"You're one to talk." She laughs and shakes her head. "Do you want to grab me a cloth?" She wipes at her face. "Oh no, I got it all over my clothes."

"Then we'd better get you out of them." I reach around her body and pull on her apron strings. It falls to the floor and she sucks in a fast breath. "This sweater, it has to go."

"Agreed," she says her voice low, breathless...aroused.

She lifts her arms and lets me peel it over her head and with one quick flick, I have her bra removed. I pick her up and turn her, setting her on one of her white marble tabletops.

"I was thinking, a chocolate-covered Josie, is probably going to be a hell of a lot tastier than anything we've made tonight." She squirms, as I go back and get the bowl with the leftover chocolate, still warm and gooey. I nudge her until she's flat on her back, and I dip my finger into the bowl, swirling it around the chocolate. Once it's thoroughly coated, I run it around her nipple, and it puckers at my touch.

I lean down and take her puckered bud into my mouth, and flavor explodes on my tongue. "Jesus, you taste good," I murmur, and treat her other nipple to that same pleasure. She writhes beneath me, and I step to the end of the table, grip her yoga pants at the waist and slide them down her long, sexy legs. I gaze at the beautiful woman on display, and my cock grows impossibly thicker. I remove her panties and tug on her until her legs are dangling over the edge. I coat my fingers with chocolate, trail them up her inner thighs and follow behind with my tongue.

"God, that is good," she says, her body quaking beneath my touch.

"So good," I murmur, and breathe warm air all over her pussy when I reach it. She grips my hair to hold me and lifts her hips, rubbing her pussy all over my mouth. I love it how she takes what she needs with me, no inhibitions, just full on honesty.

I put her legs over my shoulders and lap at her. She moans the way I like and I reward her with a thick finger. I slide it high inside her core, and her muscles ripple around me. She is so damn close. I lift my head and take in her glossy, lust-imbued eyes.

"I am never going to be able to taste chocolate again without thinking about this moment."

She goes up on her elbows. "Same." Her chest rises and falls rapidly, her gorgeous breasts beckoning my mouth again. "That's going to be hard for me, considering I work with chocolate every single day."

I remove her legs from my shoulders, and stand to unzip my pants. My cock jumps free and I take it into my hand. "Speaking of hard."

She laughs, and opens her legs for me. I step up to her, and grip her hips for leverage, as I jerk my hips forward and completely fill her.

"Brody," she cries.

"I know, Josie. I know."

This isn't just good. It's great, and what we're doing here, it isn't just fucking. No, it's so much more. Too much more for me to walk away from. Which means it's time to come clean and tell her everything. Will she walk out of my life like every other woman has, or will she put the past in the past, and begin to live to the fullest—with me.

It's time to find out.

14

JOSIE

Christmas Eve:

"I love this quaint town," I say quietly, and I take in all the twinkling lights as we drive down Main Street toward the Bradbury's home. I shift the box of bark on my lap, the sense of peace and joy inside me bringing on a smile, and memories of Brody spreading warm chocolate on my body bringing heat to my core. When was the last time I was this happy?

Beside me, Brody taps the steering wheel. "I've never seen a town go all out like this at Christmas."

I turn, a small smile still on my face as I take in Brody's strong profile. He flicks on the wipers and while I wish it was snowing instead of raining, it matters little. Nothing can spoil my light and cheerful mood tonight. I shake my head as I take in Brody's freshly shaven face. This last week has been a whirlwind of emotions, with this man breathing new life into me.

How could I not fall for him?

Okay, it's true, I've only known Brody for a short time, but I'm in love with him. At least I no longer have to lie to Patrick. I'm not sure what the future holds. Is Brody interested in a long-distance relationship. Is that even feasible? Then there's that small crack in my heart. Will it ever heal and allow me to be whole again? I have so many unanswered questions, but the one thing I do know is that I'm not ready for this man to walk out of my life.

"You're awfully quiet," Brody says, his hand sliding across the seat to capture mine. He brings it to his mouth and kisses it. My heart beats a little faster, the things I feel for him welling up inside me and shifting me off kilter.

"Just thinking," I tell him.

"Good thoughts?"

I chuckle. "Good thoughts, and Brody..."

"Yeah."

Tell him, Josie. Tell him exactly how you feel.

I take a breath, wanting to tell him, but struggle to voice the words. I'm positive it's that small unhealed piece of my heart that's preventing me from fully opening up.

"We're here." He stops the car and kills the ignition. Turning to me, he arches a brow. "What were you going to say?"

"It can wait," I tell him. Maybe tomorrow morning, when we're beneath our gorgeous Christmas tree, I'll be able to get the words out without the guilt.

"You sure?"

"I'm sure." I glance up and take in the big, decorated house. "Let's go have some fun."

I'm about to turn, but he puts his hand around my neck to stop me. I look back at him and his eyes are half shut, yet full of desire. My pulse jumps as he brings my mouth to his and lightly brushes his lips over mine, for a tender, passionate kiss that takes the breath from my lungs.

"What did I do to deserve that?" I say quietly when he inches back.

"I think I'm falling for you, Josie." My chest squeezes, and once again, I can't voice the words. Silence hovers, takes up space between us. I open my mouth and struggle to speak, say something in return. I want to desperately, but can't. "You don't have to say anything and I understand you want to move forward, but things that happened in your past are keeping you back." He laughs softly and shakes his head. "Despite all that, I went and fell for you anyway."

"Brody," I manage to get out through a tight throat, as a car pulls up behind us and headlights light us both up. I take in the want reflecting in his eyes. I lost my husband. It gutted me. I've not been able to move on, not knowing if he'd want me to or not. I might not ever hear him speak the words, and a part of me will always wonder, worry that I'm dishonoring him. I'll always love him, but being with Brody is right, in my head and in my heart.

"I have to talk to you about something." He reaches inside his coat, puts his hand into an inside pocket, but a knock on our steamy window stops him.

"Are you guys going to make out in the car all night or join the party," Declan says, his arm around Nikki.

We both laugh, and Brody reaches for his handle. I guess whatever it is he wanted to talk about, or show me, will have to wait. I can't help but wonder if it's a Christmas present. I have one for him too, and I can't wait to see his face when I give it to him. I just hope I'm not rushing this. Then again, he did just tell me he was falling for me. I can't seem to wipe the smile from my face as I exit the car, the box of chocolate bark in my hand. Brody comes around and puts his arm around me, trying to shield me from the rain as we rush up to the front door.

The warmth of the house washes over me, as Donna and Fred greet us and take our wet coats.

"Come in, come in," Donna says and smiles at me as I hand her the bark.

"A little gift from Brody and me." I flush thinking about the fun we had after we made it. "We made it together."

"You didn't have to bring anything."

"Fine then, more bark for me," Brody says and Donna slaps his hand away as he tries to snatch it back. We all laugh. "Did he really help you with this, Josie?"

"He was a great help." Brody grins at me and heat moves into my face. I have no doubt he's thinking about how we put the remainder of that melted chocolate to good use.

Donna leans in, a gleam in her eye. "Rumor has it you and Brody are an item."

"An item, Mom, really?" Declan says with a laugh.

Donna whacks him. "Stop it." She turns back to us and claps her hands. "Anyway, I'm glad the rumors were true. You two are so perfect for each other."

"I think so too," Brody says and tugs me to him. My heart soars. I can't remember the last time I was this happy.

She shakes her head and gives her son a playful scowl. "I can't believe Declan kept this from us."

"It all happened rather quickly," I say quietly when I hear Patrick's voice coming from the other room.

"Nevertheless, it happened and I couldn't be happier for you two. Now come on into the living room. Have a drink and make yourselves at home."

We follow Declan and Nikki into the living room and Declan introduces us to his family members from out of town. We greet them, and I take note of the way Declan's cousin is staring at Brody like he's a big fat snack. He might very well be, but he's my fat snack, not hers. Eugenie, I think that was her name, turns to me, and if looks could kill, holy. What did I ever do to her?

Nikki calls me over to the bar, and I excuse myself from Brody. But he's not alone for a second. Nope. Eugenie is right there, taking selfies with him.

"You two look happy," Nikki says.

I can't seem to stop smiling. "Yeah, we are. Wait, what's wrong?" I ask when I take in the sadness in her eyes.

She frowns. "The guys are leaving the day after Christmas. It's always hard when Declan leaves."

"You'll miss him?"

She smiles but it doesn't reach her eyes. "He's my best friend."

"Is that all you are?"

"Yeah," she says and I nod.

"I should probably tell you, Patrick has been asking about you."

Her head rears back. "Really?"

"I think he likes you. He's a nice guy, Nikki. I mean, if you and Declan aren't an 'item,'" I say, using Donna's words. "Maybe you should give him a chance."

"Yeah, maybe."

Something she said niggles at me. "Wait, did you say they were leaving right after Christmas?" She nods and I frown. "Brody said something about staying until New Year's Day."

"Nope, as far as I know they're leaving the day after Christmas. They have to get back to work." She looks down when she adds, "Declan probably has to get back to one of his girls for when the ball drops." Before I can say anything, she points to the wine bottles. "Red or white?"

"Red, please."

She pours me a big glass and as Eugenie laughs, the sound like nails on a chalk board, I take a huge drink. Nikki laughs. "Good thing you're here tonight."

"Why do you say that?"

"Donna doesn't let anyone come to the table without a date and if you don't have one, she finds one for you. Could be a friend, a coworker, a family member." She frowns and stares at her drink for a moment.

I touch her hand. "Hey, are you okay?"

She plasters on a smile. "I'm fine." Her gaze moves over the crowd. "It's just... Declan and I go way back, and he always asks me to Christmas Eve dinner so he's not stuck sitting with someone of his mother's choice."

My gut tightens. "Maybe he likes spending time with you."

She shrugs. "Yeah, I guess. Friends for life." She tips her wine my way. "But you...you and Brody have a good thing going." I turn and jealousy rips through me, and it takes all my strength not to cross the room and slide between him and Eugenie, making it clear he's mine.

He's mine.

As I stare at the gorgeous man who nearly put all the pieces of my shattered heart back together, something uneasy works its way through my blood. I turn back to Nikki. "Do you think Brody would have been paired with Eugenie if I hadn't come?"

"Declan told me that was the plan."

That unease mushrooms. Is it possible that I'm only here tonight, so he wasn't stuck with Declan's cousin, who can't seem to keep her hands off of him? Nah, that can't be right. Brody wouldn't do something like that. What we've shared this week was real. Right?

Then why do I have a horrible feeling careening through my blood?

Brody glances at me over his shoulder, his eyes pleading and all worry evaporates. "I'd better go rescue him," I say to Nikki, and lift up my wine glass. I cross the room and make a beeline for my man.

"Miss me," I say to Brody as I sidle in next to him.

He puts his arm around me in a show of possession, and Eugenie glares at me. I give her a bright smile as Declan's mom comes into the room and calls us all to dinner. Brody guides me to the long table that seats at least twenty people and we take our places. Eugenie is seated next to Patrick, but Patrick has his eyes on Nikki, who had an incredible sadness about her that she's trying to hide.

"Everything looks beautiful," I tell Donna and she beams. Soon enough we're all eating, and naturally the conversation turns to hockey, everyone at the table wanting to hear what's going on with Declan and Brody. I'm almost too full when dessert comes, but it's apple pie so how can I say no?

After dinner, we all head to the living room, sipping on coffee, and as I snuggle in next to Brody, sleep tugs at me. "I think we need to get you home to bed," Brody whispers into my ear, and I couldn't agree more.

We say our goodbyes and Donna and Fred hand our coats back to us at the door. Donna turns to Brody. "I assume we'll be seeing more of you around Holiday Peak."

"If someone plays their cards right, you will," he says and winks at me. I can't help but laugh, and poke him in the side, but I love his playfulness.

We head outside, and Brody walks me to the passenger side, gentleman that he is. In the car, on our way home—my goodness I'm actually calling my loft, *our* home—my phone pings. I tug it from my purse and find a message from Kayley. I text her back.

"Everything okay?" Brody asks.

"Yeah, that was Kayley, wishing me a Merry Christmas."

I lean my head back, and briefly close my eyes, a flood of emotions washing over me.

"You like your new phone?"

"I do, but..."

He casts a quick glance my way his brow furrowed. "But what?"

With my head resting on the seat I roll it toward him, and the rain comes down harder on the roof of the car. But I don't mind it. It's cozy and the sound soothes my soul. "Jon, my late..." My words fall off as a lump jumps into my throat. "He left a voice message for me on my old phone." It's hard to tell in the dashboard light, but I swear the color just drained from Brody's face. I cringe, thinking how cruel I was the day we met. He didn't deserve my outbursts, and now, from the tightening of his body, it's easy to see he blames himself. "It's not your fault," I tell him quickly. "I was the one who dropped it, long before you splashed me."

"You didn't back up your phone?"

"I tried. My laptop is so old, and it crashes a lot. I've been busy and never had time to get a new one."

"What did the message say?"

"I don't know. I could never bring myself to listen to it, and now I'll never know."

"Josie," he says, his voice low, strained, almost unrecognizable. He pulls up in front of the shop, kills the engine and he looks stricken as he turns to me. "I need to talk to you."

"Can I ask you something first?"

"Okay."

"Was I...did you...I mean, you didn't bring me tonight so you wouldn't be paired with Eugenie, did you?"

His shoulders go stiff. "Who told you that?" he blurts out, his tone full of accusation.

My heart stops beating at his reaction—or rather, overreaction. "Brody. It's a simple question."

He sucks in a fast breath and my stomach clenches. He glances down, but I already know his answer is going to crush my already fragile heart. "It's not what you think."

"So you didn't bring me to avoid being paired with Declan's cousin?"

His head lifts, and he stares straight ahead. His fingers tighten on the steering wheel, and my blood drains to my toes. I cross my arms as my body begins to shake. "Brody?"

"Yes and no. It's complicated."

I work to keep my voice steady when I say, "Uncomplicate it, then. Tell me what's really going on." Tears blur my eyes and there's a part of me that doesn't want to believe the man who cooked homemade traditional foods for me had some ulterior motive.

"It's just...I knew I'd be paired with her, and Declan challenged me."

My breath comes quicker. "Challenged you?"

"He picked you." He grips the back of his neck. "Shit, this isn't coming out right. Look, I wanted you to go with me."

My mind races, trying to figure out what he's trying to say. "Did you guys have a bet or something?" Oh God, that can't be right. We had so much fun this week, grew so close. Was that all in my imagination? Was he charming me, sweet talking me simply to win a bet and get me to the table? "Brody?" I croak out, and inch toward the door.

"It wasn't a bet." His voice is low, pained. "Not really."

I hug myself harder, as a chill seeps into my bones. "What was it then?"

"Can we talk inside?" He takes in my shaking body. "You're freezing."

I nod, my voice stuck in my throat.

He touches my arm, his entire body tense. "Let me get your door. I don't want you stepping into any potholes."

I nod again as uneasy energy courses through my veins. He circles the car, opens my door, and when he bends something falls from his pocket and lands in a puddle of icy water. "What was that?"

"Shit." He reaches into the puddle, and fishes around. He pulls his hand out and shakes it. "That's freezing."

"What did you lose?" I ask.

Without answering me, he shoves his hand into the puddle again, and after a good search he pulls his hand out, and when I see what he's holding, the world closes in on me. My throat squeezes tight, and I can't seem to get air.

"Brody?" I squeak out as my mouth goes desert dry.

"Can we talk?"

"That's...my phone. Where did you get my phone?"

"It's not what you think." He reaches for my hand but I pull it back, my mind going back to the day we met. Over the course of the last week, it occurred to me that Brody and I had so much in common. From our favorite type of Christmas tree, right down to popcorn in our bark.

"None of it was a coincidence, was it?" I ask quietly, tears pounding behind my eyes.

A garbled sound comes out of his throat. "You and me, Josie. That's fate."

"Fate." I give a hard shake of my head. "Fate didn't bring us together," I say as the pieces fall into place. "Declan brought us together. He picked me—to be your dinner date so you wouldn't be stuck with his cousin—which meant you had to pursue me." I point to my dripping phone. "Is this how you did it? You went through my phone, looked at my pictures, then did all the things I used to like doing?"

"No, Josie. That's not it. I mean, some of what you're saying is true, but it's not like that. Please, let me explain."

A hard laugh gets stuck in my throat. I snatch the phone from him and try to turn it on, but it's waterlogged, completely ruined. I toss it back to him, and jump from the car, pushing him out of my way.

"It might have been a game to you, Brody, but it wasn't to me. I hope you and Declan had fun playing with my heart."

"Josie, please."

My blood turns to ice and slowly moves through my body. "Were you even planning on staying until New Year's, or was that just another big lie to worm your way into my life and take what you needed from me."

"No, it wasn't a lie." There's a desperation about him as he reaches for me, but I jerk back. "I was going to talk to my coach, and if I couldn't, I was going to drive back up to kiss you when the ball dropped."

"How can I possibly believe that," I shoot back. "Or anything else you say?"

"Josie?"

"Goodbye, Brody." I force myself to stay calm, not to cry in front of him. He doesn't deserve my tears. "I don't ever want to see you again."

15

BRODY

I stand there, the world crashing in on me as Josie pushes past me, her dripping wet phone still in my hand. She clearly hates me now, and you know what. I hate me too. All this time I was holding onto the one thing that was precious to her, the one last chance to hear her late husband's voice and yes, it's wrong that I even considered peeking into her personal life because Declan threw up a stupid challenge. I don't deserve her. I don't deserve happiness at all. But she does. No one in the world deserves it more than Josie.

Looking at the world through blurry eyes, and it has nothing to do with the rain, I get back in my car. Not knowing where to go, or who to turn to, I drive back to Declan's. I glance at the phone in the seat beside me and once again mentally berate myself. I fuck everything up. It's what I do. I never, ever should have started anything with Josie. This is all on me.

I sit in the driveway and soon Declan's front door opens, and he walks out with Nikki. He takes one look at my car, me sitting alone in the driver's seat and turns to say something to

Nikki. She nods, gives me a little wave and goes back inside the house. The next thing I know, the passenger door opens and I snatch up Josie's phone as Declan slides in.

He takes one look at my face and shakes his head. "What happened?"

"We're done." I punch the ceiling. "Josie walked."

"Why?"

"Don't all women walk from my life, Declan?"

"Come on, Brody, there's more to it than that."

"Shit, what am I saying? This isn't on Josie, this is on me. She's nothing like my mother and stepmothers. She's way better than any of them." I exhale, pinching my nose. "This is on me, Declan. I fucked up."

"We need to fix it then."

"There's no fixing it." I hold up Josie's phone and Declan frowns. I quickly give him a rundown on what I did, and didn't do—which was invade her privacy. But none of that matters. Not really.

"Shit, this is bad. I know you never opened her phone, I know you'd never do that, but she thinks you did, and just the fact that you kept it, had it all this time..." He gives a low slow whistle. "There might not be any coming back from that, bud. But you have to at least try, don't you think?"

"I don't know what to think anymore." I shake my head, because there is no making this right. "Her phone... She needs to hear her late husband's message. She might not want to move forward with me, but I at least hope the message is what she needs to hear, what it's going to take to heal her wholly and help her find happiness, even if it's not with me."

I punch the ceiling again, the thoughts of her being with another man eating me alive. But I'll just have to deal with that. This is about Josie, not me, and I'll do anything to make this right.

"Come on, I know a guy."

"What?"

"If we want to save the phone, we have to work fast. Start the car and drive east." I do as Declan orders. "Go faster."

I drive east, and step on the gas pedal, going past the speed limit, but if he knows a way to fix the phone, I'll deal with a speeding ticket.

We pull into a small subdivision, and the houses are all lit up. "Right there, pull into the driveway."

"It looks like there's a house party." Unease tightens my gut. "We can't barge in on someone's party, it's Christmas Eve."

Declan laughs. "Are you kidding me? We bring the party wherever we go. How many people get to say two Seattle Shooters showed up at their door on Christmas Eve?"

"Yeah, I guess." I reach for the door. "If you think it's okay."

"Come on."

Phone in hand, we hurry up to the door, and Declan knocks. The door swings open and there's a middle-aged man standing there. "Declan, son, what are you doing here?" the man asks, arms wide to hug Declan. After they separate, the man's eyes go bigger when he turns to me. "Brody Tucker, what a surprise. This is the best Christmas present ever." He calls over his shoulder, "You guys are not going to believe this." He waves his hand. "Come in, come in."

Declan clears his throat. "We kind of need a favor, Mr. Ferguson."

"What can I do for you?"

Declan takes the phone from my hand. "It's damaged and we *need* it to work. We'll pay whatever it takes, and we'll be happy to give you as many selfies and autographs as you want."

Mr. Ferguson laughs as his wife comes around the corner. "Sandra, you remember Declan." She beams. "You take these boys to the living room and introduce them. I'll be back in a jiffy."

My stomach clenches, hoping this works, I put on a smile and let Mrs. Ferguson take me into the room and introduce us around. For the next fifteen minutes, we make small talk, and thankfully Declan carries the conversation. I'm too worked up to focus on anything.

We get our pictures taken, and sign autographs and soon enough Mr. Ferguson comes back into the room, a frown on his face, and my heart sinks into my stomach.

He gestures for us to follow him back into the hall and we say our goodbyes before following him. In the hall, I try to quiet my racing heart. "Not working?"

"Oh, it's working...it's just, this is Josie Moser's phone."

"You got it working!" I practically shout, my throat aching as I hold back tears.

"Yes, but what are you doing with her phone?"

"It's a long story, Mr. Ferguson. But I can assure you, we are planning on giving it back. We're planning on making everything right, isn't that right, Brody?"

"Yeah," I say, even though there is nothing I can do to make it right.

He hands the phone over. "Lots of memories that I'm sure she wouldn't want to lose."

"Yeah, exactly," I agree.

"How much?" Declan asks and pulls out his wallet.

Mr. Ferguson waves his hand. "No charge. Just as long as you get this back to Josie."

We head outside and back in the car, Declan says, "He owns the Mobile Shop in town. He can fix anything."

"Thank you, Declan. This means a lot."

"And obviously, she means a lot to you." I nod, and head back to Declan's. "Are you going to go see her tonight?"

"I'm pretty sure she won't open the door for me and I don't want to leave this on her doorstep in the dark." As much as I wanted to wake up with her Christmas morning, I know better than to go to her tonight. Distance is probably the best thing for us. The party has died down by the time we get back, and I'm happy to see that Patrick is gone. How would I explain that I'm sleeping at Declan's tonight? Declan searches for Nikki, but his mother informs him that Patrick took her home. Declan is in a foul mood as he goes to his bedroom and I follow him up the stairs, going into my own room, shutting the door and flopping on the bed. I close my eyes, but sleep doesn't come and I want to get up and out early, to put the phone on her doorstep. That way she'll find it when she takes Mabel for her morning walk.

I toss and turn until morning and rub my sleepy eyes as the light shines in through the slant in my curtains. Walking quietly through the house, not wanting to wake anyone, I head to the front door when I notice some extra gift bags. Sure that Donna wouldn't mind me using one, I drop the phone in and a cool morning breeze washes over me when I step outside. I quietly back my car out of the driveway and head to Josie's. I sit in the car for a minute, my insides twisted up, and finally force myself to put one leg in front of the other. I walk around the shop to her back door, put the bag on the doorknob, and head back to my car.

I knew better than to start anything with her and now I've fucked everything up, hurt the one woman who would never hurt anyone, and has been through so much pain herself. I love her, there's no denying that, but she'd be better off without me in her life messing everything up.

16

JOSIE

My barking dog pulls me awake. I open one eye and then the other, my gaze going straight to my gigantic tree. I'm on the sofa and the Douglas fir eats up the whole room, so it's not a surprise that it's the only thing I can see.

Wrong.

Mabel pokes me with her wet nose. "What's up, girl?" Through puffy eyes from crying, I check my phone for the time and groan. "You're up way too early."

Her tail wags and when I try to roll over, she barks and barks and barks some more. "Ugh, you're not going to let me sleep, are you?"

She runs from the sofa, through the kitchen, and barks at the back door. "Fine, I'm coming," I say, reluctantly forcing myself up. Exhaustion from a very sleepless night pulls at me as I trudge to the kitchen, pull on my boots and coat, and leash Mabel. I hate that I cried over Brody. Brody who helped with Mabel, took me on a horse-drawn carriage ride, and showed me how to live again. Brody who was using me for some stupid game between him and his best friend.

Mabel barks at me and it pulls me out of my stupor. "Okay, okay, what is your rush this morning anyway?" As she practically drags me down the stairs, I try to think about something other than Brody, but can't. Honestly, why would he invest so much time in getting to know me, doing things with me when all he had to do was ask and I would have gone with him. After all, he was doing me a favor by pretending to be my boyfriend. I guess he liked the thrill of the chase, being able to sweet talk me. Maybe it was all ego driven.

I open the door and I'm blasted with a cold breeze and Mabel tries to pull me to the road, which is so strange. "We're going to the park, girl. Wrong way." I go to close the door, and that's when I notice the gift bag on the doorknob. I stare at the bag for a moment, glancing around. I snort. "Looks like Santa came, Mabel."

I take the bag from the knob and my heart jumps into my throat when I see my phone inside. My chest squeezes so tight, it's hard to breathe, and no longer able to stand, I sink to the ground, the cold wet snow seeping through my pajama bottoms, but I'm too numb to feel anything.

I pull the phone out, and as if sensing my distress, sweet Mabel sits beside me, nudging me with her chin. Tears flood my eyes as I carefully, tentatively turn the phone on. It lights up and a big hiccupping sob crawls out of my throat. Mabel whines and moves closer, putting her head on my lap. My lungs seize, and I stop breathing when I open my messages and find the voicemail from Jon.

"Oh, God," I murmur. Mabel whines again, as if to encourage me, and I glance up at the sky, take a deep, full breath to gather my courage and press play.

"Josie, hey." As soon as I hear Jon's voice my tears fall harder, and I press pause. I hold the phone tight, not sure if I can continue but Mabel nudges me.

"Okay, girl."

I hit play again, and close my eyes, nothing existing or mattering, but Mabel and Jon's message.

"I'm not doing so great, babe." His voice is quiet and weak, barely audible from the background beeps. "They have to do surgery. Internal bleeding. I uh...I love you."

My throat squeezes so tight, it aches, and tears drip down my nose and cheeks, freezing on my skin. "Jon," I murmur. "I love you too."

"Babe, I'm not sure I'm going to be okay." He gives a soft laugh. "If I don't come out of this, I need you to be strong. We talked about having a family. I want you to do that, babe. I want you to find someone who makes you happy, someone who will love you the way I do. I want you to chase all your dreams." The background beeps come faster, more erratic, and the message ends abruptly.

I hug my phone to my heart, and let the tears fall freely. I'm sad, horrifically sad, but hearing his voice again, his words, brings a new kind of warmth to my heart, mending the last open crevice that prevented me from moving forward—the way Jon wants me to. I sit there for what feels like forever, until the sound of snow crunching beneath someone's boots reaches my ears. I glance up, just as Mabel jumps to all fours. I reach for her leash, but I'm too late. She's running and barking, her tail going crazy as Brody comes around the corner and goes completely still when he sees me sitting on the ground.

"Josie," he says quickly, worry all over his face. He glances at the phone, and sucks in a breath. "Are you okay?"

"I'm not...but I am." I run my finger over the phone. "Thank you for this."

"Declan knew a guy. He fixed it."

I nod, go quiet for a long time, then say, "I appreciate that."

He jerks his thumb over his shoulder. "Do you want me to leave?"

I go quiet again, thinking about what I want. All along, I knew Brody was one of the good guys, which is why it hurt so much to think he went through my phone. He didn't seem the type, which is why it gutted me, but if there is one thing I know, life is short and precious, and not everyone gets a second chance. In my heart, I still can't believe he didn't feel more for me. His passionate kisses, his tender, loving touch... how could that not have been real?

"Why are you here?"

"I'm sorry. I know you said you never wanted to see me again, but I forgot to put your Christmas present in the bag."

"This was the best Christmas present," I say and tuck my phone into my pocket. "I don't need anything else." That's not true. I need a lot. From the man standing before me.

"I wanted you to have this." He produces a hat similar to his, but with a pink pompom. Despite everything, I laugh.

"What did you do?"

"I got hold of Wes's mother, and asked her to make one for you. We couriered it so you'd have it for Christmas."

My heart swells, aches with all the things I feel for this man. I pat the ground. "Come sit."

Snow crunches and Mabel stays right at his heels as he closes the distance between us and sits. He puts the hat on my head and takes my hand. "You listened to Jon's message."

I nod. "Yeah."

He falls quiet leaving me to my own thoughts. After a long while, he breaks the silence. "I never went through your phone. I thought about it. But I'm not that guy."

"No, you're not."

"You believe me?"

"Yeah, I do."

He exhales, and a puff of white cloud forms in front of his handsome face.

"Josie, I want to be honest. I liked you from the second you yelled at me."

Embarrassment floods me. "Sorry, I was having a bad day and never should have taken it out on you."

"You don't have to apologize. I understand." He rubs his thumb over my hand. "The challenge with Declan was stupid and immature. He might have picked you, but you're the only girl I ever would have picked to be beside me, now and...forever."

"Forever?" I ask, and swallow.

"When I found out about your late husband's message, I…I didn't know what to do. I wanted to give you the phone but didn't want you to hate me, or think I tricked you in some way. I don't blame you for thinking that. Last night, the phone was in my pocket because I planned to confess. You see, Josie, I fell in love with you. Everything we did, said, and shared…it was real for me. When I told you I was falling for you, I meant it. It wasn't about sweet talking you into a date." A big hiccupping sob catches in my throat. "I didn't open your phone. Fate brought us together, because we're very much alike. We like the same things, want the same things."

"What do you want, Brody?"

"I want you. I want Mabel. I want us. I want a future." He squeezes my hands. "What do you want?"

I stand, brushing snow from my pajamas, the cold seeping into my bones. I hold the bag out. "You dropped this and left. Now you're back. Was it all about the hat?"

He shakes his head. "I went to my car. I was convinced that if I hurt you like that, you were better off without me and then I realized I was wrong."

"You were?"

"Yes. There isn't a man in the world who is going to worship you the way I will, Josie. I'm the man for you and while I made a stupid mistake, I plan to spend the rest of my life making it up to you."

"I made a mistake too." I turn from him and open the door.

"Josie, please," he says his voice full of fear and pain.

I glance at him over my shoulder. "Are you going to sit on the ground all day or come inside?"

He blows out a relieved breath, and Mabel barks as he pushes to his feet. We all go inside. Silence surrounds us as we step into the living room. "I made a mistake when I told you I never wanted to see you again. You're a good guy, Brody. I should have believed in you."

"What do you want, Josie?" he asks, the tree lights falling over him, creating a warmth and coziness.

I gesture to the small present under the tree. "I think you'll understand when you open that."

He slowly tears his gaze away from me, and picks up the present. "What is it?"

"Open it."

He rips into the paper and finds a small box. He pulls the lid off, and a smile lights up his face as understanding dawns. "A key to your—"

"Heart."

He smiles, pulling me to him.

"And to my place, of course," I add with a laugh. "Brody, I love you. I never thought I'd love again. Never thought I should or could, but you busted that notion all apart, helped me heal and brought me back to life. I thank you for that." Mabel barks like she's thankful too. "I've never had a long-distance relationship, and I don't know what the future holds, but all I know is I want to do it with you."

"Josie, I always embraced life, but until you I never knew what living really meant. I've never done a long-distance relationship either, or any relationship. I'm doing a lot of things I've never done before. We both are, but I'm not afraid because it's you I'm doing them with, and will figure things out day by day." He laughs. "Oh my God, that was right out of a Hallmark movie, wasn't it? Do I have to cash in my man card now?"

I laugh, nodding as I snuggle in and breathe in his warmth. I put my hand on his chest, revel in the strength of his heart as it beats beneath my hand. I'm happy. For the first time in a long time, I'm happy.

"I'm pretty sure we can figure out something better to do with your man card."

He laughs, light and joyous, as he scoops me into his arms, Mabel prancing around us, and barking with happiness. "Look at that, we really do like and want the same things." His lips find mine. "I love you, Josie. Merry Christmas."

"Merry Christmas, Brody, and I love you too."

His grin is wicked. "Show me."

* * *

Thank you so much for reading, **The Sweet Talker**, book 11 in my **Players on Ice**. I hope you loved this story as much as I loved writing it. Keep reading for an excerpt of **Fair Play Book 1, in my End Zone series.**

If you love sport romances, check out Fair Play

ELLA:

"What does this button do?"

I smack my best friend's hand away from the football's team brand new camcorder, and give her the evil eye. She knows better than to play with it, which makes the shocked looked on her face all the more amusing. But the fact is, I've been entrusted with the very expensive device to record the Falcons' first home game. Since I can't afford to replace it, I can't let my friend go around poking at every shiny knob and possibly breaking something.

"What?" Peyton says, blinking dark lashes over big innocent eyes. "I'm just asking a question."

"No. You're pushing buttons you shouldn't be pushing. Now sit there before I send you to the bleachers with everyone else." I point to the bench to the left of us and raise a warning brow.

She gives a light laugh, brushing off my threat. "You'd never do that. You love me too much." She's right. I wouldn't. Peyton and I have been best friends since kindergarten, and for the last three years we've been college roommates choosing apartment-style living over a sorority house. She's here for a degree in social work, and I'm here because I want to be a filmmaker. Yeah, working in Hollywood, behind the scenes, has been my dream since childhood.

Beside me, Peyton gives a very big, very happy sigh and takes in the football field from our perch—only the best, first class seating for the camera woman. "I do love the perks of being your best friend," she says as she admires the football players warming up. A few are so close we could practically reach out and touch them if we wanted to. I don't.

"I really can't understand the fascination," I murmur. "A bunch of guys in tight pants chasing a ball."

She crosses her arms, and waggles her brows at me. "What's it called again when a player passes the goal line with the ball in his hand?"

"Winning," I say, giving her a look that suggests she might be dense, but when she breaks out laughing, I crack a smile. Yeah, I get it. I'm the one who's dense. It's true, I know nothing about football, but I need this fourth-year credit to complete my cinematic arts degree and really, do I need to understand the game to record it for the team to analyze later? That would be a big fat no. I hope.

"Well, at least you know how this thing works," Peyton says, once again scoping out the buttons on my camcorder. "How about this knob? What does it do?"

"Peyton, cut it out." I slap her hand again and laugh at her childish antics. How we remained friends all these years when we're so different is a mystery. But we love each other like sisters. Sisters? Wait, that's not right at all. I'm an identical twin and my sister Ivy and I go together like hotdogs and Ferris wheels. Peyton and I, however, no matter how different, we just work.

I stare at her. "Don't you have football players to drool over?" Unlike me, she knows every player, and doesn't hold the same kind of grudge against them as I do.

I adjust my ballcap to shade the sun from my eyes as I glance out at the football field. I catch sight of my sister Ivy as she kicks one leg out and flirts with one of the players, trailing her finger over his chest. Blonde and bubbly. That's Ivy. We were raised by the same two parents, yet we're so different, and I wouldn't be caught dead in a cheerleading outfit that barely covered my ass. That's her business though, and I don't judge or interfere in her life, just like she doesn't interfere in mine.

I'd like to think when push comes to shove, she'd be there for me, just like I'd be there for her. At least, I think she'd be there for me. We might not hang out, but we love one another and have each other's best interests at heart. Of that I'm certain. It's funny really. Ever since we were young, we fell into certain roles. The extrovert and the introvert, the outgoing one and the quiet one. I always stood in the shadows and let her have the limelight. Pretty Ivy, the theater student who lights up a room with her smile and flamboyance when she enters. Which of course, makes me the introverted smart, quiet one. We both easily fell into those roles and have yet to stray.

Peyton gives a low, slow whistle. "I don't know what you have against tight pants. Look at all those cute butts and luscious muscles. Talk about slurpalicious." She rakes her teeth over her bottom lip. "Don't you want one little nibble, one taste?"

I give her a playful shove to move her away from the camcorder. "No. No nibbles. No tastes." I'm a virgin with no plans to change that anytime soon, and as my best friend, she damn well knows it. I take up position behind the camera, and look at the world through my beloved lens. I exhale a contented breath. This is where I belong. This is where I feel most at home.

Okay, yeah, so it's true. I'm the world's biggest nerd. Do I care? Nope. Not one little bit. I'm happy to stand in the shadow and view the world through my camcorder lens. As I do, I catch sight of Ivy again as she shakes her ass for the boys on the field. Truth be told, I actually hate football players. Back in high school, they bullied my friend Jacob until he ended up taking his own life. Terrible hazing went on at our school. The bullying was torturous and cruel, and no matter how hard Peyton and I tried to help Jacob, get him help, the bullying continued, and actually increased the more we tried to stop it. A stab of pain sears my heart at the painful memory, and I suck in air to breathe through it. I know I shouldn't lump all jocks into one category, shouldn't label them all as egotistical bullies, but a single player has yet to prove me wrong. Arrogant assholes. What more can I say?

I check my watch, as my stomach growls. "Hungry much?" Peyton says. "Maybe you'd like a nibble after all?"

"Really, Peyton. Did you just meet me?" I tease and reach into my backpack and grab a granola bar, all the while trying to cleanse my brain of football players and their tight asses—one player in particular. Peyton holds her hand out, and I place a bar in her palm. Granola bars and juice boxes on the go. The life of a busy fourth year student—or that of a toddler.

She tears into her wrapper and looks me in the eye. Her brow is furrowed as she examines me like I'm a bug under a microscope—a new kind of species no one can figure out. "You really don't find any of those guys attractive?"

"Nope, not a single one of them." A little white lie never hurt anything, right? "I prefer brains over brawn."

"That's a pretty blanket statement don't you think? I bet a lot of them are smart." Peyton doesn't hold the same grudge as I do. She figured it was a few bad apples on our high school football team who persecuted Jacob until his suicide, not every jock in the world. I don't forgive as easily. Maybe it's the social worker in her. She sees the world through a different lens, and that's her right.

"Yeah, probably." I shrug. She's right, but it doesn't matter. I'm not going to hold it against her if she wants to date a player.

She grins. "What about Landon Brooks?"

A chunk of granola lodges in my throat and I try not to react, try not to let my eyes bulge out of my brain as I choke. Reacting will only fuel her ridiculous fantasy that Landon and I would be good together. She's wrong, a million times over. A trillion, even.

I snatch a juice box from my backpack, rip the straw open and jab the foil opening. After a big sip, I roll my eyes. "Oh, Please, Landon's ego is as big as—"

"His cock?"

Ohmigod.

My granola bar jumps back into my throat and I take another huge sip. In my calmest voice, I stare at her and say, "That is not what I was going to say. I mean, come on. I have no idea how big his...his thing is, and I don't want to know."

"His *thing*." She laughs. "Oh, come on, Ella. You can say cock. I know you've watched porn before. We've watched it together, for God's sake. We all have fantasies, and that's normal."

Flustered, I say, "Okay, fine. His cock. That's the last time you're going to hear that word on my lips, and the last time I'm going to think about it." It's possible that's a lie. I might actually think of it tonight—when I watch porn.

"His cock is going nowhere near your lips then?"

I plant one hand on my hip and glare at her as she teases and twists my words. "How many ways do you need me to say it, Peyton?"

She braces her hands on the bench behind her and leans back, lifting her face to the sun. "I can tell you like him."

"I do not like him."

"What do you have against him anyway?"

Oh, other than the fact that he's living rent free in my head, nothing. "He's an asshole, and wait, why did you say his ego was as big as his cock. How do you know that?"

She gives me a slow grin that says she knows me too well. "Ah, look at that, you are thinking about his *thing* again." She wags her dark brows. "You know, they just don't call him Torpedo because he's lightning fast, on the field. It's because he has a big—"

"Stop," I say. I take a fast breath. *Do not think about Landon's torpedo*. I'm two seconds from demoting her to the bleachers, when she sits up straight, her mouth gaping. "What?" I ask, my blood draining to my toes even though I have no idea what's going on. I only know that look on her face and it's bad. So very, very bad. She looks past my shoulder and points her finger.

"Uh..."

Ohmigod. I mouth the words, "He's behind me, isn't he?"

As she gives a slow nod, I spin around. Landon is adjusting his helmet as his gaze moves over my face. He's not smirking, or showing any sign that he overheard us. Thank God!

"Hey," he says and my stupid ovaries quiver as my gaze lands on his brutally handsome face. He's not typically handsome, with a square jaw, perfect skin, perfect features. No. He's a bit harder, his face scarred from fights, and football. It only makes him hotter.

"Hey," I squeak out.

He smiles at me, then looks past my shoulder to Peyton when she clears her throat. "Hey, Peyton."

"Landon," Peyton says. "Looking good out there."

He turns his attention back to me. "Coach wants to know if you've got this thing all figured out." He gestures with a nod to the camcorder and I try not to react to his sexy Texas accent. "You know how to work all these buttons?"

"Yes, I do," I say, and while I get that he has no idea how to use the camcorder, there are plenty of buttons this guy knows how to press. Yes, I'm talking about the buttons between a girl's legs and the ones on the end of each breast. I've heard the rumors, and have zero intentions of ever finding out if they're true. I'd have a better chance of landing an assistant director position with Spielberg right out of college than this guy has of landing a position between my sheets. Not that he wants that, but chances of either of them happening: zero.

His gaze rakes over me, and my goddamn legs nearly give out as those dark eyes ignite my blood from simmer to inferno. What the hell is wrong with me? I do not like football players. I do not like Landon.

Yeah, you just keep telling yourself that, Ella.

"Wait, am I seeing double," he asks, and looks from me to Ivy and back to me again.

"Ivy is my twin," I say with an exaggerated sigh, and steal a fast glance at her across the field. As if feeling my eyes on her, her head lifts, and she stares at me. I can't see her expression from where I'm standing. I can only imagine she's in shock to see me talking with Landon. Not because I don't associate with football players, but because a nerd like me would never be worthy of his attention. She has nothing to worry about. He's all hers.

Have at him, sis.

"How come I've never seen you around before?" He shifts from one foot to the other, and I become acutely aware of his height, and of the way his muscles fill out his uniform. Does he even need all that padding? The fresh scent of soap, fabric softener, and something uniquely Landon fills my senses. It's not a bad scent. Nope, not bad at all. Which really sucks.

"I hang in different circles," I tell him and like the nerd I am, I snort, and tap the camcorder. "Cinematography."

"Oh yeah?" Dark eyes leave mine to steal a quick glance at the camcorder, and for a second he almost seems truly interested. "You're one of those audio/visual students?"

I nod and resist the urge to roll my eyes, because honestly, the fact that he doesn't know what my major is called isn't his fault. I don't know a thing about football, and I kind of get the sense he's trying to be nice, although for the life of me I can't figure out why. I'm pretty sure he's not trying to lure me to the locker room so the team can beat the crap out of me, like those boys in high school did to Jacob.

"You mean nerds?" I ask, with a raised brow, and Peyton kicks my ankle. I whimper, but don't take my eyes off Landon. God, he's so alluring, his face brutally interesting, I'm not sure I can.

Something passes over his dark eyes. A hint of sadness? I'm not sure why I suddenly feel like I've bruised him somehow. Jeez, I'd never purposely hurt anyone, whether I liked them or not.

"I never said that. I just mean…" He shrugs one of those broad shoulders and it's all I can do to keep my gaze from dropping…from admiring all his muscles. "You, uh, you like movies, huh?"

"Yes. I like movies," I respond, and resist the urge to walk through the door he just opened. Once someone brings up movies, I could go on and on about films, rambling about what I like, what I don't like, but I don't want to bore him to death. He has a game to play, women to impress.

He rubs a scar beneath his eye, and it flares red. "Seen anything good lately?"

How did he get that? Football, or something else? "Yes," I say again, and he smiles.

"Any recommendations?"

Porn.

What. The. Hell.

Get yourself together, girl!!

"Depends on what you like." I say, trying for casual when my stupid brain is conjuring up all kinds of unwanted images. Landon on top of me, underneath me...

"You should come to the party tonight." He gestures to the field with a nod. "I'll show you what I like."

Holy shit, no. He is definitely barking up the wrong tree here. I am not one of his groupies, bunnies, cleat chasers, or whatever the hell they call women who sleep with footballers. Wait! My brain takes a moment to catch up, alerting me that the guy everyone calls torpedo—and not just because he's lightning fast—invited me to a party. Did I just enter the twilight zone or something? I think I might have heard him wrong.

"I'm busy," I say.

This time his smile is cocky, full of brazen confidence, and I get it. I really do. I get why women hand their panties over. "Come on, you can't be too busy to celebrate our win?"

"Pretty sure of yourself," I say in a bored voice, even though there's a storm going on inside me.

He cocks his head. "Attitude is half the battle, don't you think?"

"You don't want to know what I think," I mumble.

He grins, and despite myself, my stupid lips twitch. God, why am I acting like a dim-witted moth around him? Yes, he's a shining star and has his own gravitational pull, but I am not into egotistical football players. My only goal is to keep my head down, finish my degree and get a job in Hollywood. Why I'm suddenly on this guy's radar is beyond me. Did he lose a bet or something? Have to talk to the nerdy girl? If not, and if there's something about me that appeals to him, he should go after Ivy. We look alike, except she dyes her hair blonde, and he could have her with a snap of his fingers.

"Her name is Ella," Peyton says. "She'll be at that party."

I spin, and give my former best friend the death glare. She studies her nails, like she doesn't have a care in the world. From across the field, a whistle blows, and I nearly jump ten feet in the air when a big, strong hand lands on my arm. I spin to face Landon, and he snatches his hand back.

"Sorry, didn't mean to touch without permission." He holds both hands up, palms out. "I just ah, I gotta go. Coach is call-ing." He pauses for a brief second.

"What?" I ask as I reposition myself at the camcorder and reach for the record button. Wait, why is it on? Rattled, and pretending not to be, as Landon continues to stand there, six feet of sex in a football outfit, looming over my small frame, I flick the record button off, and close my eyes, hoping when I open them again, he'll be gone.

"Aren't you going to say good luck?"

Nope not gone, and goddamn that cocky grin of his. I'm going to give my traitorous body—one spot in particular—a good hard lecture when we get home. With my vibrator.

"Good luck," I murmur, sounding uninterested.

He backs up an inch and I can almost fully refill my lungs again. "See you tonight, Ella."

"Not going to be there," I say.

He pauses and I sigh as I look at him. Why won't he leave already?

"How about this? If I score a touchdown, you come, if I don't…then it's my loss. In more ways than one."

His loss? Okay, I really am in some alternate universe. Football players do not flirt with me, and that's the way I like it.

"Why would I bargain with you? What could possibly be in it for me?"

"Come tonight." He flashes perfect white teeth. "Find out."

"We'll be there," Peyton says, finality in her tone, letting us both know it's going to happen and the conversation is over.

"We will not be there," I clarify through clenched teeth. We have a better chance of getting snow in Southern California this late September evening. Not. Going. To. Happen.

"See you tonight, Peyton," Landon says. "See you too, Ella." He points to the camera. "Now you'd better press record. You don't want to miss my touchdown."

My God, could the guy be any hotter...I mean, cockier. Yeah, cockier, that's what I meant. The guy is *not* hot. Nope not hot at all.

Much.

If you want to see what kind of trouble Ella and Landon get into, check it out here **Fair Play.**

ALSO BY CATHRYN FOX

The Puck Charmer

The Troublemaker

The Rule Breaker

The Rookie

The Sweet Talker

In the Line of Duty

His Obsession Next Door

His Strings to Pull

His Trouble in Talulah

His Taste of Temptation

His Moment to Steal

His Best Friend's Girl

His Reason to Stay

Confessions

Confessions of a Bad Boy Professor

Confessions of a Bad Boy Officer

Confessions of a Bad Boy Fighter

Confessions of a Bad Boy Doctor

Confessions of a Bad Boy Gamer

Confessions of a Bad Boy Millionaire

Confessions of a Bad Boy Santa

Confessions of a Bad Boy CEO

Hands On

Hands On

Body Contact

Full Exposure

Dossier

Private Reserve

House Rules

Under Pressure

Big Catch

Brazilian Fantasy

Improper Proposal

Boys of Beachville

Good at Being Bad

Igniting the Bad Boy

Bad Girl Therapy

Stone Cliff Series:

Crashing Down

Wasted Summer

Love Lessons

Wrapped Up

Eternal Pleasure Series

Instinctive

Impulsive

Indulgent

Sun Stroked Series

Seaside Seduction

Deep Desire

Private Pleasure

Captured and Claimed Series:

Yours to Take

Yours to Teach

Yours to Keep

Firefighter Heat Series

Fever

Siren

Flash Fire

Playing For Keeps Series

Slow Ride

Wild Ride

Sweet Ride

Breaking the Rules:

Hold Me Down Hard

Pin Me Up Proper

Tie Me Down Tight

Stand Alone Title:

Hands on with the CEO

Torn Between Two Brothers

ABOUT CATHRYN

New York Times and *USA today* Bestselling author, Cathryn is a wife, mom, sister, daughter, and friend. She loves dogs, sunny weather, anything chocolate (she never says no to a brownie) pizza and red wine. She has two teenagers who keep her busy with their never ending activities, and a husband who is convinced he can turn her into a mixed martial arts fan. Cathryn can never find balance in her life, is always trying to find time to go to the gym, can never keep up with emails, Facebook or Twitter and tries to write page-turning books that her readers will love.

Connect with Cathryn:
Newsletter https://app.mailerlite.com/webforms/
landing/c1f8n1
Twitter: https://twitter.com/writercatfox
Facebook: https://www.facebook.com/
AuthorCathrynFox?ref=hl
Blog: http://cathrynfox.com/blog/
Goodreads: https://www.goodreads.com/author/show/
91799.Cathryn_Fox

Pinterest http://www.pinterest.com/catkalen/